BANSHEE

Books by Margaret Millar

NOVELS

THE INVISIBLE WORM
THE WEAK-EYED BAT
THE DEVIL LOVES ME
WALL OF EYES
FIRE WILL FREEZE
THE IRON GATES
EXPERIMENT IN SPRINGTIME
IT'S ALL IN THE FAMILY
THE CANNIBAL HEART
DO EVIL IN RETURN
VANISH IN AN INSTANT
ROSE'S LAST SUMMER
WIVES AND LOVERS
BEAST IN VIEW
AN AIR THAT KILLS
THE LISTENING WALLS
A STRANGER IN MY GRAVE
HOW LIKE AN ANGEL
THE FIEND
BEYOND THIS POINT ARE MONSTERS
ASK FOR ME TOMORROW
THE MURDER OF MIRANDA
MERMAID

OTHER

THE BIRDS AND THE
BEASTS WERE THERE (AUTOBIOGRAPHY)

BANSHEE

Margaret Millar

WILLIAM MORROW AND COMPANY, INC.

New York   1983

Library of Congress Cataloging in Publication Data

Millar, Margaret.
  Banshee.

  I. Title.
PS3563.I3725B3   1983   813'.54   82-22848
ISBN 0-688-01897-1

Printed in the United States of America

First Edition

1 2 3 4 5 6 7 8 9 10

BOOK DESIGN BY ELLEN LOGIUDICE

To Carol and Ralph Sipper

BANSHEE

Chapter ONE

The princess skipped down the garden path accompanied by her court. The larger of her two attendants had thick black hair and allegedly came from Newfoundland but this was never proved. The other was a brown-haired German. Both were loyal and affectionate (though frequently inclined to ignore commands that seemed impractical or unnecessary) and both listened attentively. Newf's fat silky belly made a soft pillow for the royal head when its owner wished to lie under the oak tree and watch the little worms twisting and turning at the tips of the leaves like high-wire performers in a circus.

Shep too was very useful. He pulled the royal roller skates around the driveway and licked dirt and blood off scraped knees and elbows so the princess wouldn't have to go inside the house and be fussed over. Shep did just as good a job as the housekeeper, Mrs. Chisholm, with her washcloths and soap and cotton balls dipped in alcohol. Moreover, Shep's tongue was very gentle and didn't sting.

Mrs. Chisholm was always suspicious, of course. "Looks to me like somebody had another fall, that's how it looks to me like."

"I don't hurt," said Annamay, admitting nothing while not actually lying.

"Bet a dollar to a doughnut that's what happened. And you let one of those creatures spit all over you again. One of these days you'll perish from some dread disease carried by dog spit."

Mrs. Chisholm frequently lost points by exaggeration, hitting the ball so hard it landed in another court and her opponent won by default.

"If *I* were your mother I'd send samples of dog spit to a laboratory to be tested for pernicious germs. Maybe I'll do it on my own."

"No, you won't, Chizzy."

"And pray, why not?"

"It might cost a lot of money. They might charge you for every single germ. And what if they found a million of them at a penny each?"

Chizzy did some quick arithmetic and retreated with dignity. "I would send the bill to your father."

The princess continued on down through the cutting garden, past the lath house and the koi pond to the palace which had been especially built for her. The palace had seemed enormous at first but every year it shrank until now there was hardly room, when her attendants were allowed inside, for Annamay to entertain friends and look after her favorite children.

Both children required skilled care. Marietta had lost half her hair, not to some dread disease but to Newf who finally upchucked most of it in the vegetable garden along with one of Luella Lu's glass eyes. Luella Lu's eye, miraculously intact, was retrieved, washed and glued back in place but it remained fixed in its socket while the other eye moved, and Luella Lu ever after looked quite mysterious, as though she could see things others couldn't. A repentant Newf often carried her around in his mouth by way of apology and there were no hard feelings within the royal circle.

Not many princesses managed without a maid but Annamay did. She cleaned and cooked, she entertained her friends and Chizzy and her mother and father and their friend Benjamin who had designed the palace. She served peanut-butter sandwiches and orange juice. On these occasions Newf and Shep had to be evicted to make room for the guests. They would stand outside peering into the windows, drooling and reproachful. Although the dogs didn't care for peanut-butter sandwiches they were strong on principle and it seemed patently unfair for them to be excluded from the palace merely to make interlopers more comfortable.

Sometimes the princess, disguised as a commoner in shorts and T-shirt, went off adventuring. These excursions usually started down by the creek below the avocado grove. Here, while the dogs ate avocados, seeds and all, Annamay caught tadpoles and water walkers. She picked canyon sunflowers the color of her hair and periwinkles the color of her eyes, and practiced jumping from shore to shore.

In one of her storybooks a little lost boy had followed a creek downstream because he knew that eventually it would lead to civilization. And sure enough it did, not only for the little lost boy but for Annamay, who ended up at the Cunninghams' swimming pool.

Mr. Cunningham was lying on a canvas mat stark naked. Annamay had never seen a naked man before and it was quite interesting what with one thing and another. Then Mr. Cunningham grabbed a towel and wrapped it around his waist.

"What do you mean creeping up on me like that, you crazy kid?"

"I wasn't creeping," Annamay said. "I was following the water downstream seeking civilization."

"Well, you sure as hell came to the wrong place."

Mr. Cunningham stretched, yawned, scratched his pink glossy scalp. Annamay wondered if he had been born with his hair in the wrong places which would make him, in Chizzy's vocabulary, one of God's little mistakes.

"There are," he added, "savages lurking behind every tree."

"I don't see any."

"There wouldn't be much point in their lurking if you saw them."

Mr. Cunningham's mother called out from the house, "Who is it, dear?" She sounded quite drunk, not surprisingly so since Chizzy said Mrs. Cunningham had a great thirst. "Who is it, Peter dear?"

"The Hyatt girl."

"What does she want?"

"Civilization."

"How peculiar."

"I don't want civilization," Annamay said. "I was only testing the story about the lost boy going downstream and coming across civilization."

"Next time," Mr. Cunningham said, "try going upstream."

Sometimes the princess had unexpected callers, like the bearded man with the tambourine strapped to his back. He was stealing avocados but came up to the palace to see if a midget lived there.

The dogs barked at him furiously but just as furiously wagged their tails, so the man wasn't scared until Chizzy came charging down the path waving a broom and shouting. Every living creature in the neighborhood was afraid of Chizzy with or without a broom because she had, according to Annamay's father, Howard, a voice that would shatter glass. The prospect of such a delightful occurrence kept Annamay at Chizzy's heels for several days after she received this information. But no glass was shattered except by Annamay herself when she helped with the dishes.

The bearded man came again later in the week, but not right into the grove or up to the palace where he could be spotted from the house. He stayed down by the creek and took off his shoes and let the water run over his feet. Since this was precisely what Annamay and Newf and Shep liked to do, it was almost inevitable that they should all meet.

12

Paws and feet dangled companionably in the water.

"What's that thing on your back?"

"A tambourine."

"Why?"

"It is a tambourine because that's what it was destined to be."

"I meant why do you carry it around? Does it make music? Do you have to take lessons and practice?"

"No lessons or practice. No music either. It makes a noise when you shake it. Shake it a little bit for soft, a lot for loud."

He was almost as hairy as Newf with his long beard and moustache and thick bushy eyebrows.

"Why do you want to make a noise?"

"To attract attention."

Annamay couldn't understand this since she herself had all the attention she could tolerate, what with parents and relatives and Chizzy and the teachers at school. "Do you like attracting attention?"

"It's a necessary part of my system. It brings me an audience. Then I predict something weird and they all think I'm loony and they give me money to go away because I make them uncomfortable."

"It's like pesting, sounds to me."

"Similar."

"What's your name?"

"You can call me grandpa."

"No, I can't. I already have two grandpas, one here and one on Long Island. So I'd better call you something else, like your name for instance."

"Okay, how about Mr. Cassandra?"

"Is that your really truly name?"

"Close enough. It's my spiritual name. Everyone has many names. They come and go like the tides. On Mondays, I am called Harold."

Annamay was beginning to feel uneasy, so she put her

sneakers back on. At this signal both dogs stood up and Newf shook his head back and forth, sending spit flying several yards in each direction.

"See?" the man said. "My system even works on kids and dogs."

The avocado grove had two seasons. In winter the Fuertes ripened, with their shiny smooth skin still green. In summer it was the Hass variety with rough black skin and fruit that spread like butter. Annamay couldn't understand why people laughed when her father referred to the place as half Hass ranch, and when she repeated it at school the teacher bit her lower lip as though she were trying to prevent it from smiling.

Summer brought the most visitors, not only because the fruit was more luscious but because there were more hitchhikers along the freeway linking San Diego to San Francisco. The hitchhikers were often hungry and they came to pick up windfalls from the ground or even pluck the fruit right off the trees. Annamay never served avocados when she entertained because she thought they tasted like the face cream her mother kept on her dressing table.

One of the hitchhikers, a girl, must have shared Annamay's opinion for she seemed much more interested in the palace than in the fruit. While the man with her filled his backpack and pockets, the girl walked around the palace smiling, touching. Annamay had learned about babies at school and from her cousin Dru and so she knew there was a baby growing inside the girl, who kept saying, "Oh wow, look at this, Phil. Real electric lights and an honest-to-God barbecue pit. I wonder if some child actually lives here."

"No," Phil said. "It's probably a playhouse for some spoiled brat."

Annamay stepped out the door and announced in a regal manner that she was not a spoiled brat but a princess.

"No kidding," the man said. He was pale and very thin,

probably from some dread disease Chizzy would know about. But he had a nice smile and a heart tattooed on his forearm. "So where's your crown?"

"Princesses don't wear crowns except on festive occasions."

"This is festive enough for me. I'm eating."

The girl laughed and said, "Don't tease her, Phil. She's a doll, simply a doll."

In the light of Marietta's missing hair and Luella Lu's glued eye and tooth-marked limbs this was a dubious compliment. But the girl's tone had been admiring and Annamay blushed modestly. "No, I'm not."

"Hey, do you mind if we take some of your avocados?"

"You already did."

"Oh, so you're a smart one too. All right, do you mind if we take some more?"

"*I* don't mind—"

"Gee, thanks a heap."

"—but Chizzy does. Because of the root rot."

This warning might have had little effect on the young couple if Chizzy hadn't suddenly appeared on cue. She came rushing around the side of the lath house carrying a hoe and screaming blue murder. Chizzy's voice sent birds fluttering out of trees and cats slinking away from gopher holes and the young couple tearing off down the hill. The girl fell at the bottom and cried out and the young man had to pick her up and carry her across the creek. He wasn't very big to begin with and he staggered under the load of a backpack filled with avocados and woman filled with child.

"Chizzy, are we rich?"

"Richer than some, not as rich as others."

"Why don't we let people come and eat the avocados?"

"Because."

"I hate becauses."

"Becauses are necessary."

"Why?"

"Because," Chizzy said, looking pleased with herself.

Then she explained for about the fiftieth time about root rot and how strangers coming into the grove might carry the fungus on their shoes and all the trees would sicken and die.

"Could the girl give root rot to her baby?"

"Yes, and to you too, if you don't stop talking to strangers. Where are the dogs? They're supposed to be protecting you."

"I commanded them to chase the garbage man."

Chizzy wiped her face with her apron and made an exasperated little noise that sounded like a towhee in the underbrush. "Oh, I'll be glad when summer's over and you're back in school. All this worrying and scurrying after you is too much for a woman my age."

"How old are you?"

"Older than some and not as old as others."

The dogs returned, doubly smug because they had obeyed a royal command and at the same time rid the neighborhood of a scoundrel who stole garbage.

"What did I tell you about talking to strangers?"

"The same as always."

"Why, I even made up that poem. Took me the better part of two nights and I bet you don't even remember it."

"I do so."

"All right then, recite it, word for word."

It was a very bad poem with unpredictable rhythms and rhymes but Chizzy was extremely proud of it and loved to hear it recited.

> Do not talk to strangers
> No matter whether they smile.
> Never accept a ride from anyone
> Even for half a mile.
> Never take money or brownies
> Even if they're homemade,

Because the money is probably laden with germs
And the brownies might contain a razor blade.
Run away fast
Or this day might be your last.

Annamay recited the poem, making only two mistakes, while Chizzy listened, her eyes moist with pride. She dabbed them with a corner of her apron.

"It's not much of a poem," she said deprecatingly. "But it packs a wallop. Nobody who hears it will ever forget it." Then she recited the final lines in a deep doomsday voice:

"Run away fast
Or this day might be your very last."

"What if I have a broken leg and can't run away because of the heavy cast?"

"You don't have a broken leg."

"Or maybe a sprained ankle."

She didn't have a broken leg or sprained ankle, she didn't run away, there was no stranger.

Annamay's favorite visitor was Benjamin York. Perhaps because he had designed the palace to begin with, he played the royal game to the hilt. Calling himself the Duke of York, he always bowed deeply when he entered the palace to give the princess a token of affection from her loyal subjects. He often stayed for afternoon tea or a rousing game of old maid or snakes and ladders. His losses at these games were so frequent that eventually Annamay became suspicious.

"You're cheating, Benjie."

"Cheating, Your Highness? Now why would anyone cheat to lose? People cheat to win."

"Not you."

"Forsooth, I am deeply humiliated by the accusation and I feel I deserve an apology."

"Oh bull."

"You mustn't say that."

"My cousin Dru says it all the time."

"Your cousin Dru hears it all the time. You don't."

"Well, I can't see what's the matter with it. It's just like saying *oh dog* or *oh cat.*"

"Then say oh dog or oh cat."

"I prefer bull. It sounds righter to me."

"It sounds wronger to everyone else," Ben said. "So cut it out, kiddo, or Chizzy will smack the royal butt."

"She says it too."

A compromise was finally reached. In return for a tin of Almond Roca, Annamay crossed her heart and hoped to die that she would in the future say oh cow instead of oh bull.

She never hoped to die, Benjie was no stranger, the Almond Roca contained no razor blades.

The events of the week had, as a matter of course, to be reported to her cousin Dru. She wasn't encouraged to spend the night at Dru's house because Dru's mother, according to Chizzy, carried on something fierce and was already on her third husband. But visits during the day were allowed.

The two girls swung on the glider in Dru's patio, eating chocolate-cream wafers. Probably as a result of the fierce carrying-on, Dru was very sophisticated. She disparaged Annamay's encounter with Mr. Cunningham in the buff as routine and boring.

"You are such a chee-ild," Dru said. "Of course you'll grow out of it in time. Maybe."

Dru was more impressed by the account of the man with the tambourine and his idea that people should have a different name for every day in the week. The girls made a list of names with the first letters corresponding to those of the days, Misty for Monday, Tess for Tuesday, Wendy, Tanya, Francesca, Sandra and Sunny.

Dru was also interested in the man with the heart tattooed

18

on his arm and the girl with the baby inside her. But she was skeptical of Annamay's reporting.

"How do you know there was a baby inside her? Did she *tell* you?"

"No. But she was fat."

"Lots of people are fat. Not all fat people go around having babies. I bet you don't even know where babies come from."

"I do so. The man plants a seed in the woman."

"How?"

"Well, I guess he might hand it to her like a pill and give her a glass of water so she can swallow it."

"Oh my God, you're ignorant. A woman has other openings besides her mouth."

"You mean she gets—well, like a sort of enema?"

"No, stupid. Not that opening, *the other.* Now do you understand?"

"Oh sure," Annamay said, not wanting to put any further strain on Dru's patience. Dru was inclined to pinch when she was annoyed and Annamay thought it best to change the subject entirely.

"Chizzy says we should never talk to strangers."

"That's a lot of bull," Dru said brusquely. "I'm ten now. In another year or two I'll be wanting to go steady and how am I going to meet somebody to go steady with if I don't talk to strangers? You're at that awkward age when I bet you're not even thinking of going steady."

"I don't have to."

"Why not?"

"I'm going to marry Benjie when I grow up."

"Holy moly, you don't think he'll wait for you, do you? Vicki says he's got women stashed all over town."

"What does that mean, stashed?"

It was uncharacteristic of Dru to admit any doubt. "It means standing in line ready to marry him. One of these days he'll weaken and pow, it will be all over, he'll get married like everybody else, Vicki says. Vicki's an expert on marriage. So if you don't want to end up an old maid you'd better start talking to strangers."

"I can't."

"Why can't you?"

The only adequate response to this was Chizzy's poem. Annamay recited it with gestures.

"Do not talk to strangers." Annamay shook an admonishing finger. "No matter whether they smile." She smiled evilly.

Dru was annoyed. "Oh stop that stupid playacting and just recite the poem."

Annamay began again.

> "Do not talk to strangers
> No matter whether they smile.
> Never accept a ride from anyone
> Even for half a mile.
> Never accept money or brownies
> Even if they're homemade.
> The money is probably laden with germs
> And the brownies might contain a razor blade.
> Run away fast
> Or this day might be your last."

"I never heard of brownies with razor blades in them," Dru said, sounding so irritated that Annamay moved out of range of a possible pinch. "My fathers all use an electric razor. Can you imagine a brownie big enough to contain an electric razor? Chizzy is full of bull."

"Run away fast," Annamay repeated, imitating Chizzy's doomsday voice. "Or this day might be your last."

There were no brownies containing razor blades, there was no money laden with germs, no stranger in a car.

20

Chapter TWO

The police came and went, came again and left again, throughout the summer. And toward the end of fall the funeral was held.

The small coffin was covered with camellias and white heather and here and there a bunch of cornflowers because they were the color of the princess's eyes. The church was filled to capacity. Relatives and close friends sat in the front pews on the left, and on the right neighbors and Howard Hyatt's business associates, and at the back on both sides were the well-wishers and the curiosity seekers and people who'd followed the long search in the newspapers. Also near the back were some who wanted to make sure they could get out quickly if necessary—Mrs. Cunningham with her son, Peter, on her right, and Ben York on her left. He had designed the Hyatts' house as well as the princess's palace and should have sat up front as a close friend. But he was afraid he'd break down in public as he had so often in private.

Peter Cunningham's reason was different. He had allowed his mother only two double martinis before leaving their house and he thought that would hold her. But more and more people kept filing into the church and the music kept playing on and on and finally Mrs. Cunningham began to fidget. Her fingers wriggled in her lap like fat pink worms trying to escape their jeweled collars.

"Peter dear, do you suppose I could just slip out for a minute and—"

"No. It was your idea to come in the first place."

"The music's depressing me. I need a couple of Valium."

"No."

"Not even one?"

"No. And the music is fine. Debussy. *Pavane for a Dead Princess.*"

"What's a pavane?"

"A dance."

"A dance? What an odd choice."

"Not if you feel like dancing."

"That's a naughty remark, Peter."

"Ugly," Peter said. "Evil. In poor taste and gross. But naughty? No, I think not. Try and avoid using that word in connection with anything I do, will you, old girl? It bears connotations of cuteness and I never do anything cute."

"Sometimes you do."

"Never. Comprennez?"

"Of course I comprennez." She glanced at him reproachfully, then turned her attention back to the music. "One expects Bach or Mozart. Pavane for a dead princess, indeed. She was a little snoop. Do you remember the time—?"

"Yes."

"You don't suppose there were other times, that she ever *saw* anything? Do you?"

"No."

"I really do need a Valium, Peter dear. Please?"

"No."

"Someday you will regret this, Peter. Someday it will be *my* funeral and you'll be sorry."

"Maybe. Maybe not."

"I am in great despair and pain," Mrs. Cunningham said. "And I'm beginning to hyperventilate."

Benjamin, on the other side of her, could see her bosom

heaving under layers of maroon silk. The little gold curls dangling from her maroon satin hat like Christmas ornaments had started to quiver and the silver bracelets on her arms clinked like the chains of a prisoner.

Prisoner, Benjamin thought.

There was no prisoner. No one had been arrested or even detained for very long though hundreds had been questioned, everyone who lived in the neighborhood or worked there or had reason to come to deliver mail or newspapers, to read meters or to service water softeners, to sell cosmetics or religion; migrant fruit pickers, registered sex offenders living in or passing through town, even a self-styled holy man who claimed to live only in the past and in the future. After sampling the food and accommodations at the county jail he conceded he knew nothing of the future, remembered only a few fragments of the past and preferred to spend the present on the outside rather than the inside. He went back to banging his tambourine and panhandling along the beach-front, and the death of the little princess remained a mystery.

Her parents, Kay and Howard Hyatt, sat in the front pew with Howard's father. It was the old man who insisted on a formal funeral. So Kay, who understood the depth of his grief, allowed the small bones to be wrapped in the blue down-filled comforter from the child's bed and placed inside the coffin.

The bones weighed seven and a half pounds. Benjamin was with Kay when she heard this news and it was the last time he saw her cry.

She sobbed against his shoulder. "Oh dear God, that's what she weighed when she was born."

Ben had cried too. Seven and a half pounds at birth, seven and a half at burial. It was a crazy coincidence but there was a certain rightness about it also, like the closing of a circle.

* * *

The captive worms in Mrs. Cunningham's lap still struggled to escape.

"I've started to fibrillate, Peter," she said. "Feel my pulse if you don't believe me. Fibrillation can be very dangerous."

"So stop doing it."

"I'm not doing it deliberately. I can't help it. I've always had this tendency—"

"I know all about your tendencies," Peter said.

"Why are you so cruel to me, Peter? I'm hyperventilating and I'm fibrillating and you won't even let me have a Valium. I could be cruel myself if I wanted to."

"Try it."

"There are some things you think I don't know about. But I do. And I could tell people if I wanted to. I could tell a great deal."

"Go ahead."

"Of course I won't. I'm not capable of cruelty. I just don't have it in me."

"What you have in you," Peter said, "is enough booze to float an oil tanker and enough pills to choke a herd of whales."

"You shouldn't speak like that to your mother. No son should speak like that to his mother."

"Maybe I'll start a trend."

"You made me leave the house with only one tiny drink."

"Two."

"Both seemed very weak."

"They were doubles."

"You contradict me all the time."

"No," Peter said. "Only when you lie."

Benjamin turned and said, "Sssh," not loudly, but directly into Mrs. Cunningham's left ear.

Shrinking away from him as if he'd blown poison gas at her she clasped her son's arm. "Peter, that man told me to ssssh."

"Then why don't you?"

"I consider it very rude for a stranger to address me in such a manner, especially when I'm fibrillating."

"Maybe he doesn't know you're fibrillating. Let him feel your pulse. He's not, by the way, a stranger."

"*I've* never seen him before. He must be one of *your* friends."

Peter raised one carefully trimmed eyebrow. "No. No, I think not."

Benjamin had met the Cunninghams casually at a number of social functions. Mother and son always arrived together, both elegantly and rather formally attired, Peter in dark vested suits or dinner jackets, Mrs. Cunningham in silks and brocades and velvets, jeweled and perfumed and elaborately coiffed. Their arrival usually created a stir. Peter at fifty was a handsome man, with his silver wig and deep bronze tan, and Mrs. Cunningham still showed traces of beauty. Throughout any social affair Peter remained the same but Mrs. Cunningham seemed to be struck by a series of inner earthquakes and aftershocks that loosened her coiffure, dislodged hairpins and left little gold curls dangling helplessly by their gray roots. She staggered and clutched at people to retain her balance. ("Oh, I'm *so* sorry. This frightful migraine has made me quite dizzy.") She bumped into furniture, dropped glasses and spilled food down the front of her dress. ("How clumsy of me. I seem to have lost my contact lenses.") And she departed early, leaning heavily on the arm of her son. Peter never appeared embarrassed or angry, merely rather amused as though he'd been playing a walk-on role in some dreadfully amateur drama.

"If he's not one of your friends," Mrs. Cunningham said, "and he's not one of mine, who is he?"

"An architect."

"We don't need an architect, do we?"

"No."

"Then I don't have to pay any attention to him when he tells me to sssssh, do I?"

25

"No. So I'll tell you. Shut up."

The music stopped and the Reverend Michael Dunlop began to speak. His training and years of experience seemed to be forgotten. His voice was not the one he used in Sunday sermons to teach, exhort, inspire or downright terrify. This voice was uncertain and so soft it was barely audible in the back rows. He had officiated at hundreds of burials but the deceased had been old or ill or had died in accidents or by their own hands. Annamay Rebecca Hyatt was eight years old and she had, in the words of the coroner's jury, died at the hands of another.

He was angry, baffled. He questioned his faith and the wisdom of God, the competence of the police and the motives and veracity of his audience. He paused between sentences, almost as if he expected someone might stand up and confess to the crime or at least to the suppression of evidence.

"And we entrust to Your loving care the soul of this beautiful child who eight years ago was christened at this very altar, Annamay Rebecca Hyatt."

He paused again. There were coughs, sobs, sniffles, but no confession. He wanted to accuse, to threaten someone with the wrath of God, the fires of hell and eternal damnation. But he didn't believe in hell, and he had no power or right to threaten anyone, no reason to believe there was a murderer in the audience, or a murderer's friend. But he had an almost overpowering feeling that there was: *One of you did something, knows something, and by God, I'd like to force it out of you—*

His wife, Lorna, sitting in her usual place on the aisle in the middle row, was sending him her special Look which indicated he was making mistakes, saying things he should have omitted and omitting things he shouldn't have. Lorna was a good Christian and an even better critic. She was paying careful attention so she could tell him afterward what mistakes he had made in delivery, content and demeanor.

Lorna was always eager to help people improve, especially him.

He would hear about it all later, probably just before dinner which was his lowest point in the day and, maybe not coincidentally, Lorna's highest. "What's the use of speaking, Michael, if you cannot be heard by everyone in the church?" ... "Goodness me, you sounded emotional. You can't afford to have feelings, you're a minister." ... "And those long pauses when you seemed to be trying to establish eye contact with somebody. It says in the book you're never to do that. Why did you?"

Why? he thought. *Why indeed?*

Lorna wouldn't understand that he was looking for a murderer or a murderer's friend. She would consult her book and find that it was against the rules.

Lorna had a valuable book which was unknown and inaccessible to anyone else. She consulted this book frequently and, like a good friend, it offered words of wisdom which exactly matched her own opinions. Many people were puzzled by her references to the book, thinking she meant the Bible. And in a sense she did. It was her bible, anyway.

He was certain that Lorna's book would have murderers listed in the index:

MURDERER: Avoid contact with, referring to, trying to find—

By now he must have broken every rule in Lorna's book but he no longer cared. He paused between sentences, his voice trembled with emotion and he established eye contact with Annamay's father, Howard Hyatt. They were the same age, thirty-seven, and had attended the same college. Even then they moved in different social circles. Howard was president of the students' council and a business major who after graduating had joined an investment firm owned by his father and took over the management of the firm when his father retired. Howard was, in brief, a success.

Success was a big item in Lorna's book.

SUCCESS: breeds crime;
    chances of successful man entering kingdom of heaven nil;
    love of is root of all evil;
    muck and money are twin companions;
    et cetera.

The references would stretch as far as Lorna's memory and imagination. Meanwhile, success notwithstanding, he and Howard remained friends. Howard came to church a dozen or so times a year, sent his daughter, Annamay, to Sunday School and contributed generously to the building fund. And it was to Michael that Howard came after Annamay disappeared, not seeking comfort, which was impossible, but seeking an explanation of how God could let such a thing happen. Michael didn't know. He pulled out a few old saws like God writing straight with crooked lines, but he was unconvincing and unconvinced. There was no explanation.

Four months later Annamay's bones were found a mile or so up the creek under a pile of forest litter covered by a tangle of poison oak. The poison oak was red with autumn by that time and very pretty.

"I've failed you, Howard," Michael said. "I'm sorry. If I had enough faith I could give you—"

"No, you couldn't give, I'm not taking. The time for praying and pleading and groveling, all that's over. What I want now is action. And let's leave God out of it, for Christ's sake."

"The police have done their best."

"Their best isn't necessarily my best."

"What are you going to do?"

"Start over."

"Maybe I can help."

"Maybe you can."

28

The eyes of the two men met and agreed: It was time to begin. Except for a few small bones missing from the left hand and probably carried away by some animal or bird, the bones were intact and offered no evidence of how the child had died. Various theories were advanced, some reasonable, some bizarre, all of them shot down:

She had tripped, hit her head on a boulder, become unconscious and unable to call for help. This was negated by the absence of fractures or indentations on the skull.

She had stumbled headfirst into the creek and drowned. But the creek was running very low by that time and at least twenty feet from where she was found, a distance not easily covered by a drowning victim.

She had been struck by a bolt of lightning. Electrical storms, however, were rare in the area at any time of the year, especially summer. None had been reported within a thousand miles on the day she disappeared.

She had wandered into a patch of poison oak and because she was highly susceptible to it she had died there on the spot. Chizzy shot down this last theory: "Why, she'd never go near the stuff. She knew how dangerous it was, and I'd taught her and her cousin Dru how to tell it from the wild blackberry vines. I composed a poem for the girls to memorize and made them say it over and over: Of shiny leaves in three, you must careful be."

She hadn't drowned, broken a leg, been overcome by poison oak or struck by lightning. She had, in the words of the coroner's jury, died at the hands of another, a person or persons unknown.

Person or persons unknown. Michael's eyes searched up and down the aisles, back and forth along the pews like feeble twin lights trying to probe too dark a forest.

Person or persons, you are unknown but you are here. I feel your presence. I'm going to find you.

He saw his wife, Lorna, waving a handkerchief in front of her face. Observers might think she was merely fanning herself because she was too warm but Michael recognized it as one of her more meaningful signals indicating that he was, according to the book, making a fool of himself.

He thought that she might be right and how little difference it would make one way or another. There had been a time for Lorna. Now there would be a time for Annamay.

Behind Annamay's parents and grandfather and Chizzy, her cousin Dru sat with her mother, Vicki, and her current father, John Campbell. Dru was almost as big as her mother and a good deal more sensible.

Dru wanted to go home. She didn't bother asking her mother who could never make a decision on the first try. She put it straight to John. He was a large informal man several years younger than his wife, and Dru treated him more like a brother.

She pulled at his sleeve. "I want to go home, John."

"Me too."

"Why can't we?"

"Because your mother's a little squirrelly. She thinks the experience will help you mature."

"I wish she wasn't into Experience," Dru said wistfully. "It was more fun when she was into Pollution and we marched in protests and carried signs and things."

"I missed that period, fortunately. I'm no good at carrying signs."

"I could pretend to have a fainting spell," Dru said, "and you could help me get outside."

"Wouldn't work."

"Why not?"

"Face it, kid. She knows all the tricks. She probably invented most of them."

"Vicki says we're supposed to *feel* Annamay's soul. I don't. Do you?"

"Not keenly."

"How are people supposed to feel a soul?"

"Beats me," John said and chewed the moustache he'd grown to make him look older. The upper part of his moustache was blond and the bottom, where it was wet, was brown. It made him look, in Dru's opinion, uneven.

"If I chewed myself like that," Dru said, "I'd get holy hell."

"What makes you think I don't?"

"I scratch my head a lot, though."

"Why?"

"It itches."

"Good reason."

"Do *you* think I could feel Annamay's soul?" Dru said anxiously. "I don't know where to start. It would help if I knew what souls did. Do you suppose they just sort of flutter around like birds, only invisible? Maybe if I listened real hard I could feel her soul fluttering its little wings."

"Maybe. Why don't you try?"

"I'm scared. I guess I don't really want to hear it fluttering."

"Neither do I particularly," John said. "But let's give it a chance. You listen hard, I'll listen hard."

Dru closed her eyes tightly and listened very hard. But all she could hear was the minister talking and Vicki sniffling into a piece of tissue and Annamay's grandfather, sitting directly in front of her, whispering. Whispering and whispering, as if he were telling himself secrets.

Howard Hyatt reached out and touched his father's clenched hands. "Are you all right, Dad?"

The old man didn't answer. His eyes remained fixed on the small coffin, as fixed as the glass eye of Annamay's doll Luella Lu which he had glued in for her himself.

"Dad?"

"Why wasn't it me? I'm old, living is a burden. It should have been me. It was my turn. Why did He take Annamay when it was my turn?"

"Stop that now. You'll make it harder for Kay."

"But it was my turn, Howard, you know that. There has been a serious miscalculation. When I was running my business a gross error like that could not have occurred, and if it had, would have been severely punished. No one seems to be in charge anymore. Oh, I realize you think I'm irrational at times, Howard, but not now, not about this. It was *my turn*."

"Don't, Dad."

"The whole operation has been poorly run. Seniority was ignored and people were taken out of turn. Those are the key words, Howard. Seniority and turn. I am an old man and it was my turn."

"We'll discuss it later, Dad."

"There wouldn't be any point in a discussion. The whole thing has been fraudulently mismanaged from the beginning. When your mother died it was bad enough. But this, *this*—"

"Later, Dad," Howard said. "Please."

The old man had been going downhill for a couple of years and Annamay's death had accelerated his decline. He confused God and the President, the Twelve Apostles, the Supreme Court and the members of the cabinet and the board of directors of Bethlehem Steel.

He made grandiose plans to go to Moscow and Peking, London and Berlin, to straighten out misunderstandings which would never have happened if a good businessman had been in charge in the first place. Lesser plans, like dental appointments and visits to the doctor, were often abandoned as trivial, or simply forgotten.

He wrote notes to himself on bits of paper and backs of envelopes which Kay and Chizzy were always coming across in odd places throughout the house.

Fertilize roses.
Avoid eating pizza.

Future of jojoba oil? Ask McPherson.
Buy valentine for Annamay.
Remind Howard re aviatronics merger.
Tell Chizzy not to sing in kitchen. Or elsewhere.
Newf and Shep need grooming.

Howard was very patient with his father. Kay was occasionally sharp. She thought his lapses of memory could be controlled if he really tried. And so he tried. But the more he tried the more he failed, and the more he failed the more impatient Kay became.

Chizzy and Annamay were his chief allies. Chizzy knew he couldn't help forgetting; Annamay didn't care. What he forgot wasn't as important as what he remembered, what he did. He tied excellent knots in things, he repaired doll furniture, cleaned dogs' ears and removed foxtails from their paws. He played Grand Duke at royal parties in the palace and listened to Annamay's dreadful renditions of Minuet in G and *Dance of the Hours* on the piano. He would clap his hands and say, "Splendid, splendid." Since Annamay had no talent at all for music and consequently no idea how many wrong notes she struck, she was only slightly surprised at her grandfather's appraisal.

"I must have improved," she said. "The teacher told my mother last week that I had a tin ear."

"What nonsense. Neither of your ears looks the least bit like tin to me."

"Don't you think the *Dance of the Hours* sounded a little funny in spots?"

"In a few spots, perhaps. But by and large it was a fine performance."

During the weeks following Annamay's disappearance, Mr. Hyatt fell into a routine. He left the house early in the morning with the two dogs at his heels, and spent the day wandering around the property, usually within sight of the palace. The palace itself had been sealed by order of the

Sheriff's Department and no one could get inside. But the old man and the dogs waited patiently, as if they expected the princess to return at any moment with stories of her royal adventure. When the bones were finally found and identified, Mr. Hyatt had to explain to Newf and Shep that the princess would not be coming home again.

"She would if she could, of course. You both know that. It is the result of shoddy management at the top level. Fair and honorable business practices have been cast aside. Annamay was taken instead of me."

Newf wagged his great plumed tail as he always did at the sound of a human voice no matter what the words, and Shep licked the tears from the old man's face the way he used to lick Annamay's scraped knees and elbows.

At sunset the three of them trudged slowly back to the house. The dogs were hungry by this time but the old man had to be coaxed by Chizzy into eating even a small bowl of cereal or half a piece of toast.

"You'll waste away," Chizzy said. "Why, already you're hardly more than skin and—"

She bit her tongue but it was too late. The old man began to cry again. He pushed the bowl of cereal away and went up to his room to lie on the bed with his face to the wall. Of all the tears shed, his were the bitterest. They offered him no relief; they blistered his eyelids and puckered his skin like brine. He told Howard he'd been turned into a pillar of salt, and explained how this happened:

"It should have been Lot's wife who was turned into the pillar of salt as in the Book of Genesis. But the head of the salt-mining company made a gross error. He must be replaced, Howard."

"I'll see to it," Howard said.

"You're a good boy, Howard."

"Yes, Dad."

"And Kay is a good girl too. She forgets things but then once in a while I do myself. . . . Does Kay know I love her?"

"I think so."

"I'm glad to hear that. It's a mistake to keep love a secret. I used to tell Annamay I loved her and she would tell me she loved me back twice as much. And then I would say I—well, it was like a little game, Howard."

"Keep your father quiet," Kay told Howard in a voice that was becoming more steely every week. "It's for his sake we're going through this charade."

The months of waiting had aged her. Nights of violent dreams, days of horrible imaginings had dulled her lively blue eyes and stooped her shoulders and dissolved the flesh from her frame as though she were biologically degrading like the body of her only child. Her pretty blond hair looked stiff as straw. Even when she forced herself to smile the corners of her mouth wouldn't turn upward. She appealed to no one for help or counsel. In bed at night she turned away from Howard and lay as lifeless as Marietta and Luella Lu in their bunk in the palace.

"You must come to me, Kay. You must let me comfort you, love you."

"There isn't anything left in me to love."

"You're my wife. I'm cold and lonely, I need to have you lying close to me."

"I'm lying close to you."

"I want to love you, Kay. Have I lost my wife as well as my child?"

"I don't know."

The person who tried hardest to bring the two together was Ben York. He'd expected them to cling to each other in such a crisis. When they didn't, he begged Kay to be more loving and advised Howard to continue waiting with compassion and understanding. He appealed to Kay's older sister, Vicki, who said Kay was terribly spoiled, always had been, and needed a course in deprivation like *est*. Old Mr. Hyatt's explanation for the rift varied, but the same theme was repeated: One of the top executives had pressed the wrong button.

When Ben tried to talk to Kay and Howard together they regarded him like a stranger caught in the act of robbing their house, a bungling pathetic amateur.

"You've never been married, have you, Ben?"

"Not exactly."

"Then butt out."

Ben had known the Hyatts for a long time. Howard had given him his first job while he was in college, and arranged his most important assignment after he graduated from architectural school. His reputation was solidly established after he designed the Hyatts' own house and the princess's palace. He was considerably younger than they were but sometimes he felt like their older brother and sometimes like their son. He even had occasional dreams of living in the palace himself, and he would wake up contented and refreshed as if he'd been on holiday at a happier place and time.

From his seat in the back row he had glimpses of Howard at the front sitting with his father on one side and Kay on the other, and beside Kay, Chizzy. This was his family, his only family, and he very much wanted to be sitting with them as they'd asked him to do. But he didn't trust his own emotions, so he sat near the rear exit, mute, suffering, smothering in the fumes of Mrs. Cunningham's perfume.

"Do you know," Mrs. Cunningham said, "what fibrillation is?"

When she repeated the question, Ben realized that she was addressing him and not her son. He responded with a shake of his head. "No, I don't."

"It means a very, very rapid beating of the heart. It can be extremely dangerous, often fatal. I am fibrillating right this minute."

"I'm sorry to hear it."

"You don't happen to have a Librium or something on that order, do you?"

"No. Sorry."

"People don't go around prepared the way they used to. In my day I never went anywhere without smelling salts, for instance. They had an odor like lavender but they contained something like ammonia that could knock you for a loop."

"I see."

"Now whenever I go out my son searches through my handbag to make sure I'm not carrying anything of that nature, not even a wee drop of booze for use in an emergency like this. A very small amount of bourbon or scotch would tide me over if you—"

"I don't have any."

She frowned at him through the little maroon veil that reached to her cheekbones and the bridge of her nose. "I don't understand why people go about unprepared."

"Maybe because they don't know what to be prepared for."

"They must be prepared for the worst because that's what happens."

"Amen," said the Reverend Michael Dunlop, and went over to the coffin and placed both his hands on the lid and bowed his head. People thought he was praying because what else would a minister be doing beside a coffin with his eyes closed, his mouth moving? But he was not praying; the words his lips formed were not part of any liturgy.

"Good-bye, dear child. Your murderer will be found, will never be forgiven or forgotten, will never spend a single day without torment. I swear this to you, Annamay Rebecca Hyatt."

Without opening his eyes he was aware that Lorna was standing beside him. He could hear her angry rapid breathing and then her voice, whisper-soft but still managing to sound urgent:

"What on earth are you doing, Michael? This isn't what's supposed to come next."

"What's supposed to come next?"

"You say a prayer aloud asking for the salvation of her soul and pleading for mercy for the perpetrator of the deed."

He opened his eyes and gave her a look of such intense hatred she stepped back, holding her purse across her chest like a shield. "That's what you did when Mrs. Vallancourt was hit by a truck and the driver was never found. Then after the plea for mercy you led the procession of mourners past the body. Why aren't you doing that now?"

"There is no body. There is a pile of bones."

"Stop repeating that. I want to remember her as she was, whole and pretty and—"

"Seven and a half pounds of bones," he said.

Chapter THREE

On a bluff overlooking the sea, Annamay was buried in the Hyatt family plot. Granite headstones marked the graves of those already there, Howard's mother, and his older brother and his wife who'd been killed in a plane crash.

"Don't you worry," Mr. Hyatt told Kay. "Grandma will take good care of Annamay just the way she did of me. You mustn't fret that she'll be neglected."

Kay pressed his arm. "Thanks, Dad."

"She never let me miss a meal or go out in the rain without my umbrella.... It seems to me it never rains anymore, Kay. Did you notice that?"

"The rains will start soon."

"Aristophanes had something quite blasphemous to say about rain but I can't remember what it was. Did Chizzy make the right kind of sandwiches?"

"You'd better ask her."

He asked her and Chizzy said, well, yes and no. She'd made a few peanut-butter for him and Dru but the rest had to be fancier for Vicki and her husband and Ben and the Reverend Dunlop.

"But Annamay never served anything but peanut-butter."

"Now you stop fussing here and now. If Mrs. Hyatt were still alive she'd give you one of those sharp looks of hers and you'd shut up like a clam."

The old man was pleased. "She could stare down the devil himself, couldn't she? I don't mind admitting I used to shake in my boots sometimes."

"You can start shaking again right now because Miss Vicki is giving you the eye. That means she's fixing to make one of her speeches if you don't be quiet."

"God forbid."

"Him and me too."

Vicki was not, in fact, paying any attention to the old man. She was watching her daughter, Dru, with critical appraisal. Dru, who'd inherited her father's mousy brown hair and gray eyes, was not turning out as pretty as she'd hoped. If she was to make a good marriage she would have to be taught some of the charming little graces that came naturally to Annamay. Dru was devastatingly direct. She bossed her boyfriends, beat them at games, and if they still had any doubts about their inferiority she put it to them in blunt language. She treated her stepfather, John Campbell, with equal candor and she didn't mind in the least when she was treated back the same way.

"I think I see a whale," Dru told him.

"What kind?"

"Gray."

"Wrong time of year," John said. "The herds of gray don't pass here on their way to Baja until late winter or early spring."

"Maybe this one is independent and decided to go ahead on his own."

"Her own."

"You can't tell if it's a female all the way from here."

"If a whale decides to be independent and louse up the whole routine it's a her."

"I guess you're right," Dru said fairly. She had few illusions about either sex or any species.

"On the other hand," said John Campbell who could be as impartial as Dru, "I must point out that females often make excellent leaders. When a flock of pintails or widgeon flies by, it will be a female at the head of it. And among predators like hawks and owls the female is about one-third larger and much fiercer."

"I'm going to be big like my father, aren't I?"

"Very likely."

"Oh well, I don't care. Maybe I'll be a professional basketball player, maybe the world's first girl champion slam dunker."

"I'll come and cheer."

"Why did you marry my mother?"

"I'm not sure." He looked across the open grave at Vicki who was standing with Kay and Howard waiting for the casket to arrive. "She's pretty and cute. Also, she asked me."

"Did she really really truly ask you?"

"Yep."

"You could have said no."

"I didn't want to."

He had met Vicki through his job at the Museum of Natural History. She was into Conservation at the time and was taking a course in marine biology. She often stayed after class to ask questions and she appeared so interested in the subject that he would take her down to the beach to make on-the-spot studies of tide-pool life. He would remove a starfish clinging to a rock or a sea urchin half buried in the sand, show her how each one functioned, then replace the specimen carefully where it belonged. She listened with wide-eyed fascination. By the time he discovered that the object of her fascination was not inside but outside the tide pools, it was too late. Her previous husbands, daughter, succession of lovers, didn't matter.

"Do you suppose," Dru said, "that she also asked the others?"

"I wouldn't be surprised."

He seemed amused at the idea and looked across the grave at his wife and met her eyes and smiled. She was indeed pretty and cute even if she hadn't learned a thing about sea urchins.

The hearse arrived and four of the mortician's assistants brought out the casket. All through the church service Dru had avoided looking at it. Now she couldn't help it. There it was, and underneath the camellias and heather and cornflowers was Annamay, her dearest friend and most gullible confidante. Uttering a little cry of protest Dru ran over to her mother and threw her arms around her.

"I don't want any more Experience. I want to go home."

"Why, baby," Vicki said, hugging her daughter. "I had no idea you were going to be upset. I thought it would be an enriching experience."

"I don't want to be enriched."

"All right. You go wait in the car. John, give her the keys, please. You can unlock the car, can't you, Dru?"

"I can *drive* the car," Dru said.

John handed her the keys and whispered in her ear that she wasn't to drive any farther than L.A. because there was only half a tank of gas. He looked as though he wished he were going with her.

"Lock the doors and windows," Vicki said. "And if a strange man comes anywhere near, start blowing the horn."

"Why couldn't I just drive away?"

"Because you're only ten years old and—oh, for God's sake, do as I say without arguing for once."

"The horn won't blow unless I turn on the ignition."

"All right, then start screaming."

"If the windows and doors are closed nobody will hear me."

"Then just *sit there,*" Vicki whispered fiercely. "Stop this nonsense. You're ruining Annamay's funeral."

"She doesn't care. She's not here."

"Split, kiddo," John said and gave her a friendly whack on the butt.

The casket was lowered into the ground and the Reverend Michael Dunlop threw in the first handful of earth.

"We all must die," he said. "Of dust we are made and to dust we shall return."

When it was over, the family and Ben York went to the Hyatts' house for some of Chizzy's coffee and sandwiches and cake.

Dru and old Mr. Hyatt carried their plates down to the palace while Vicki took John to the garage to see the new car Howard had bought Kay to cheer her up. The car talked. The doors said, *I'm open,* the lights, *I'm on,* the gas tank, *I'm getting empty.* Even the speedometer issued a stern warning, *Slow down.*

Kay wasn't cheered. She turned away from the car as though it were a bribe, and went on driving the old station wagon she'd used to take Annamay and her friends on outings to the beach and zoo, to Disneyland, Sea World and Marineland. People talked at her, told her the new car was marvelous and she ought to be grateful and why didn't she drive it to Carmel or La Jolla for a weekend. She paid no more attention to them than to the synthesized voices that came from the car.

Vicki thought the voices were really neat though she was quick to point out one disadvantage as she and John sat in the front seat:

"What if we were making love and we heard someone say, that's illegal? What would you do?"

"I'd finish making love," John said. "And then I'd hire a lawyer."

Vicki giggled and kissed him on the side of the neck. "Oh dear, I guess we'd better go back inside."

"Why?"

"We're supposed to be offering our condolences, saying all the correct things."

"I can't think of anything more to say than I've been saying for the past four months."

"Still, it doesn't seem right that we're out here together like this, happy and everything. Does it seem right to you?"

"Nothing's a hundred percent right in a fifty percent world."

"You don't think we should be—well, suffering more?"

"It wouldn't help them any."

"Oh, John, you're so sensible."

"I'm learning from Dru," John said with some truth.

Dru was feeding chocolate cake to the goldfish in the lily pond behind the palace. The pond was an exact replica of the larger one beside the main house, and the fish in it looked like babies of the huge colorful fish in the other pond, which were called koi.

Annamay had given names to all the smaller fish and firmly believed that each one knew and responded to his or her own name. Dru refused to buy such nonsense. The fish all looked alike, so if you called Lancelot and one of them responded, it wasn't necessarily Lancelot, as Annamay always thought. It could just as well be Lucretia or Charlemagne or Beauregard. None of them liked chocolate cake very much.

"I venture to suggest," the old man said, "that they prefer fish food."

"Annamay and I tasted fish food once. It hasn't got much flavor."

"Apparently that doesn't bother them. It's reasonable to assume that taste was originally a condition of survival. What tasted good to a creature was good and what was unpalatable was bad. That doesn't hold true anymore, alas, or we would all be sitting around eating strawberry shortcake and cream puffs."

"And french fried potatoes and rocky-road ice cream."

"Not to mention pecan pie."

"And tacos and pizza and brownies." She paused, frowning. She frowned with her whole face. Her eyebrows met, her forehead wrinkled, her mouth squeezed into a straight line. "No. No, not brownies."

"Why not?"

"Because of the poem Chizzy wrote."

"I find it hard to imagine Chizzy as a poet. And brownies are surely an odd subject for a literary effort."

"It wasn't actually about brownies, it was about strangers who offered you rides in their car and money and brownies. Only the brownies might have razor blades in them."

"People are writing poems about nearly everything nowadays but brownies with razor blades in them is surely stretching it a bit. Do you remember how it goes?"

"Yes, but I'd rather not say it out loud."

"I'd like to hear it. It might alter my perspective on Chizzy."

"But it might also make you feel bad, thinking about Annamay and strangers and things."

"It might, yes. Yes. You're right, of course."

He closed his eyes and twin tears rolled down his cheeks like tiny crystal balls, balls too brief and brittle for any fortune-teller to read.

"Don't cry," Dru said, and gave him a kindly pat on the head. He had quite a lot of hair that was real, not a wig like Mr. Cunningham's. She could see his scalp shining through in places, pink and smooth, and she wondered why scalps, which didn't matter because they were usually covered with hair, never got wrinkles, and faces, which mattered a great deal, did. It was an interesting question but she didn't intend asking anybody. Vicki's answer would be immediate and connected in some way with one of Dru's misdeeds, and John Campbell would use the occasion to deliver a mini-lecture on birds or snakes or whatever.

"You're a nice little girl," Mr. Hyatt wiped his eyes with the back of his hand. "Are you as nice as Annamay?"

"No," Dru said bluntly. "I was nicer than I am now when I was her age and still innocent. Maybe she would have changed too."

"Not Annamay, no. Never."

"Everyone has to grow up."

She didn't realize until she heard the words what a terrible mistake she'd made because Annamay would never grow up.

"I'm sorry, Mr. Hyatt. I'm awfully sorry."

But it was too late. The old man was fleeing, half running, half stumbling, along the flagstone path to the house, his hands pressed against his chest as if to stem the flow of blood.

"Holy hell," Dru said, and dumped the rest of the chocolate cake into the lily pond.

Only the three of them were left in the sunny birch-paneled family room, Kay and Howard and Ben. Chizzy had gone back upstairs as soon as she'd made the coffee and sliced the cake. She felt an ominous sadness in the air, not just a sadness for the past but for the future, as though an important decision were about to be announced. Nothing had been said to her about such a decision so she was powerless to alter it no matter how deeply it would affect her. Under normal circumstances she would have eavesdropped and, hearing a word here and a word there, put them together into a sentence. But there was no such thing as normal anymore and there never would be again, and she talked brusquely to herself in the bathroom mirror: "Don't go dreaming. If there's ever any normal again it will be a new one and you'll have to get used to it, like it or not."

Ben shared none of Chizzy's premonitions. Now that the funeral was over he expected Kay and Howard to grow closer to each other again. Howard would continue to manage the investment firm, Kay would resume her job as a volunteer driver with the Red Cross, and he, Ben, could go back to his own work.

His current project was designing a pavilion for a Hollywood actor who knew exactly what he wanted, a house made entirely of windows and mirrors, no expenses spared and to hell with earthquakes. The actor's wife wanted a blue tile roof and an indoor-outdoor swimming pool.

Ben hated the assignment. People who claimed to know exactly what they wanted often didn't like the results and the money-is-no-object crowd had a tendency to ignore their bills, assuming perhaps that money was also no object to the plasterers and cement finishers and plumbers and carpenters.

But his real assignment, first and foremost, was to bring Kay and Howard together.

"I think you two should take a trip in the new car. Drive up the coast route to Big Sur and San Francisco and Point Reyes. Keep on driving. Chizzy will take care of things here and I'll drop in on Mr. Hyatt every day and take him wherever he wants to go."

Kay didn't even look at him. She was watching Howard who was pouring himself some bourbon. "What do you think of that, Howard?"

"Of what?"

"Benjamin has planned a trip for us to Big Sur and other points north. Does that appeal to you?"

"I don't believe so."

"You could always talk to the car if you got bored with my company. Or we could take turns talking to the car. Would you like that?"

"No."

Kay turned to Ben. "You see? Howard and I have become very direct with each other. No unnecessary amenities, just the straight stuff, yes and no."

"Don't talk like that," Ben said. "Stop it right now."

"I'll stop talking like that if you'll stop planning our future for us," Kay said. "Howard and I have something to tell you and you're only making it more difficult. I know you're fond of us, Ben, and you want us to stay together and live happily ever after and all that. But it's impossible."

"Only because you're not trying hard enough."

"Perhaps we don't want to try."

"But you've got to. Look at it mathematically. Neither of you alone is half of what you are together. And what's going to happen to Chizzy and the old man and the dogs and the koi?"

"The koi," Kay said. "The *koi,* for God's sake."

"And the house? *My* house? I lived and breathed this house. I love every inch of it."

"Build one of your own. That new girl who's living with you, what's her name?"

"Quinn."

"Miss or Mrs.?"

"I never asked her."

"My goodness, we *are* getting sophisticated, aren't we?"

"Quinn happens to be my assistant," Ben said stiffly.

"Really? Well, I'm sure she assists you in one way or another. Anyway, I've heard she's a beauty. Why don't you marry her, design a house of your own?"

"I don't want to get married. And I can't afford to live on a scale like this."

"It's a little unfair for you to insist we stay married when you won't even get married in the first place. Don't you think so, Ben?"

"Surely there's no question of a real divorce."

Howard finished his drink. "There'll be no drastic change at all for the moment. I'll move into the guesthouse so my comings and goings and telephone calls won't interfere with Kay's life. I expect to be pretty much absorbed in my new job."

"Your new job? What are you trying to tell me? What about the investment firm?"

"It can get along without me for a while. I have more important things to do. . . . Are you sure you wouldn't like a drink, Ben?"

"What important things?"

"Michael Dunlop and I are going to work together."

Ben looked incredulous. "You're taking up some kind of religious activity?"

"It's a religion to me by this time though it can't be called a religious activity."

"What can it be called then?"

"Michael and I are going to find the person responsible for Annamay's death."

Ben went over and opened the door that led into the main patio. He drew in a deep breath of air and held it. He felt almost faint and wished he had some of Mrs. Cunningham's smelling salts with their scent of lavender and shock of ammonia. He said finally, "So you're into that again."

"He was never out," Kay said. "Never for one single second. People like you and Dad and Vicki have been blaming me for the split in our marriage. I went along with that. It seemed easier to accept the blame than to put it on someone already overloaded with guilt. . . . He never stopped thinking about it, right from that very first night when Annamay failed to come home. Even when we lay beside each other in bed his obsession was like a tangible wall between us. When he asked me for love he meant sex, and I'm not a hooker. Would you agree with that, Howard?"

Her husband gave her a bleak little smile. "Oh yes. It's pretty obvious you're not a hooker."

"So you see, Ben," Kay went on, "this isn't a sudden decision. It was made months ago and nothing you can say will change it. Now if you don't mind I'm going up to my room. I need to be alone for a while."

The two men watched her leave, interested less in her exit than in avoiding each other's eyes.

"Okay, I get the picture," Ben said. "But why Michael Dunlop?"

"Michael and I are old friends."

"You and I are also old friends. Why didn't you pick me?"

Howard had been dreading the question and trying to prepare answers to it. But when he spoke them aloud they sounded as if he were reading from a cue card. "Your work won't go on without you like mine and your hours aren't flexible like Michael's. You have to earn a living."

"That's not the real reason, is it?"

"Partly."

"Is it because you think I'm too young, you don't respect me?"

"You're an artist, Ben. You're temperamental and emotional and—well, you're just not cut out for the kind of job this is going to be. You're not tough enough."

"I'm healthy and I stay fit. I play handball. I'm taking karate lessons."

"That isn't the kind of tough I mean. Tough is when you've seen everything, all the things a minister like Michael is forced to see. Or tough is when your only child has been murdered."

"I want to be in on the investigation."

"You will be. We'll consult you from time to time, ask your advice and so on."

"Sure," Ben said. "Sure."

"Now your feelings are hurt, aren't they? It's a good example of what I was talking about. You're too emotional. You overreact."

"I can control myself perfectly well."

"Then start now by facing the fact that Michael and I are going to—"

"Mike should stick to the Lord's work, dammit."

"Come on, Ben. There's a very important role in this for you."

50

"What do I get to do—carry a spear? Make coffee?"

"Pay extra attention to Kay. In spite of the way she talks she's very vulnerable and depressed. She doesn't have this desire for revenge that keeps me going. She's not interested in revenge, or in anything else either at the moment, and I can't help her. That's where you come in."

"Oh goody, here's where I get to make the coffee."

"Take her out to dinner when you have the chance, maybe even drive down to L.A. for a play or a concert. That is, if your Miss Quinn doesn't object."

"Miss Quinn doesn't belong to me any more than she did to the last twenty guys."

"Then you'll go out of your way to be nice to Kay?"

"I've always been nice to her. I love her. I love her like a sister." He paused for a moment. "Or maybe not like a sister. I'm not sure. Maybe I'll try to move in on you, Howard. How would you like that?"

"There you go, overreacting again. Are you actually trying to make me jealous? Don't be silly, Ben. I trust you completely."

"You might be wrong. I consider Kay the most beautiful and desirable woman in town."

"Well, don't tell me that, tell her," Howard said. "She needs it, I don't."

"What you need, pal, is a swift kick in the ass. And when I finish my course in karate I might give it to you."

"I'll be waiting. Meanwhile, will you take care of Kay? Go places with her, keep her as busy as possible. Don't let her sit around the house and brood. You could even take her out dancing. I bet you're a good dancer."

"Why do you bet that?"

"No particular reason. You seemed like the type who's a good dancer."

"There, that's another sign of the lack of respect you have for me. In that classy world of yours, men who are good dancers are considered suspect. Right?"

"I didn't—"

"Well, it so happens that I'm a lousy dancer. My feet are too big and I can't keep time. . . . Now I suppose you think I'm overreacting again, don't you?"

"It occurred to me," Howard said dryly.

"You're wrong. I was simply responding to what I consider an implied insult."

"No insult was intended. I was merely suggesting, hoping, in fact, that you might be a good dancer because Kay likes to dance and I'm very bad at it."

"Well dammit, I *am* a good dancer. Tell that to your friends at the Forum Club."

"I doubt they'd be interested. We mainly discuss politics."

"That would be way over my head, of course."

"Sit down, Ben."

"Why?"

"You might think more clearly in that position."

Ben sat on the edge of the copper-hooded fire pit that dominated one corner of the room. The season for fires hadn't arrived yet and last winter's ashes had long since been hauled away. Ben had tried to explain to Chizzy that fire pits were supposed to have ashes in them to look as if they had just been used the previous night. But Chizzy said ashes merely looked sloppy and went right on keeping the fire pit as spotless as one of her own skillets.

"You're being a problem today," Howard said. "I was hoping you'd be more of a solution."

"I will be. I'll help you and Michael with your investigation."

"That's not the kind of help I need."

"Okay, okay. I'll take Kay to dinner and out dancing, she'll fall madly in love with me, ask you for a divorce and marry me. How's that for a scenario?"

"Full of holes. You're like a son to Kay and me. Rather a bad boy at times, like right now, but we still love you. Reverting to childish behavior is your way of handling grief, I suppose. Kay's is to retreat. And mine—well, mine is to get the hell out there and fight."

Chizzy's way was to cook.

During the past few weeks she had made stews and casseroles, bread, pies and cakes, a fat turkey and scrawny little game hens. The freezer was filled and still she kept on cooking. In order to cope with the surplus she had to do a great deal of eating. Kay scarcely touched her food and Howard and his father had always been picky eaters.

Ben was of some help. He was usually hungry since none of the women who lived with him from time to time had much interest in cooking. But even he couldn't keep up with Chizzy's output.

And so she gained weight and, hating her new image, ate still more to comfort herself, and gained still more. She weighed almost as much as the two Japanese gardeners, Mitsu and Suki, put together. The young man who came to clean the pool and jacuzzi twice a week began calling her Mrs. Five by Five and didn't stop until she hit him over the head with one of his own skimmers.

Meanwhile the food kept multiplying like some prolific new form of life that couldn't be controlled. Chizzy was forced to use more drastic methods of disposal. She sent casseroles over to Dru's house, pies and cakes to Mitsu's wife and sons and to Suki's parents. She even personally delivered a meat loaf to Mrs. Cunningham down the road.

Mrs. Cunningham looked quite astonished. "What did you say this was?"

"A meat loaf."

"You mean, to *eat*?"

"Yes. To eat."

"Are you sure you came to the right place?" Mrs. Cunningham raised her voice. "Peter dear, did you order a meat loaf?"

"No one ordered it," Chizzy explained. "I'm giving it to you."

"To eat?"

"To eat."

"How extraordinary. I don't believe anyone has ever given me a meat loaf. Is there anything wrong with it? It's rather rude to ask that, I know, but now and then when there's something a wee bit wrong with something one gives it to someone else hoping they won't notice."

"There's nothing wrong with it," Chizzy said roughly. "And if you don't want it I'll take it back again."

And she did. She took it home and fed it to Newf and Shep who found nothing wrong with it at all.

It was almost dark when she appeared at the door of the family room to invite Ben to stay for dinner.

"We're having something you specially like, Irish stew with dumplings."

"Sounds great," Ben said. "But somebody is expecting me at home."

"Some woman, I suppose."

"Actually she's my assistant. I'm teaching her to read blueprints."

Chizzy sniffed and said, "Since when does an architect hire an assistant who can't already read blueprints? I can't possibly eat a whole pot of Irish stew all by myself."

"No, but I'll give odds that you'll try."

"We can build a fire and I'll leave the ashes right here in the pit, won't go near them with a ten-foot pole. And for dessert—"

"Some other time, Chizzy," Ben said and smiled at her, the kind of smile that every woman interpreted in her own way. To Chizzy it meant he would have liked nothing better than to stay and eat Irish stew but duty called and he was forcing himself to go home and face the rigorous demands of his assistant. To Howard he said, "May I have one last word?"

"Go ahead."

"Do you think the sheriff is going to appreciate a couple of amateurs horning in on his investigation?"

"No."

"And how far do you suppose you'll get without his cooperation?"

"Farther than I am now, which is nowhere."

"I don't like the sound of this," Chizzy said. "No sir, I don't like it one bit. I want to know what's going on." She tugged at the sleeve of Ben's coat like an anxious child. "You mustn't let Mr. Howard do anything dangerous."

"I have no control over him," Ben said. "I'm his little boy. . . . Right, Dad?"

He waited a moment for a reply. When none came he let himself out the back door, slamming it behind him.

Chizzy listened disapprovingly to the sound of his old Porsche roaring down the driveway. "I wish he'd buy a more respectable car. That thing makes enough noise to wake the— Oh dear. Oh *dear.*" She sagged against the wall as if her bones were dissolving. "I didn't mean to say— Oh dear, I could bite my tongue out."

"It's all right, Chizzy. Forget it."

"This is a terrible day, the worst day of my life. Worse even than when Chisholm walked out on me for that redhead with the cast in her eye. At least then I had someone to blame. But today, today I don't even have anyone to blame."

"I'll find you someone," Howard said. "I'll find you someone to blame."

Chapter FOUR

One of the members of Michael's congregation was a woman who worked as a secretary for a deputy sheriff. Esther Garrison knew Annamay and her parents by sight and after the child's disappearance she'd come to talk to Michael several times to put into words some of the doubts Michael himself was having.

Most of the cases that crossed Miss Garrison's desk concerned people who were, in some way or another, involved with evil—the victims and the victimizers and all the human links between them, the vicious and greedy, the sick, weak, dim-witted, the alcoholics and drug addicts and their pitiful debris. No evil had ever touched Annamay, and yet here she was in Miss Garrison's files, and it shook the secretary to the very foundations of her faith.

The immunity she had developed throughout the years deserted her, leaving her as vulnerable as some of the people in her own files.

Esther Garrison was a hardheaded, hardworking woman who commanded respect and wielded considerable power. No one called her by her first name, no one told her jokes or confided secrets, no one even asked her for donations. She wore all her clothes as though they were uniforms. Her sharp little eyes behind the steel-framed spectacles made people uncomfortable. They seemed to be tabulating faults and relaying them by blinking in Morse code to some mysterious consort. On those occasions when she was called to court as a witness she delivered her testimony in such a clear positive voice that no judge or jury member could doubt her.

None of the court people would have recognized the pale disheveled trembling woman who appeared in Michael's office to ask for guidance.

During the past few weeks Michael had noticed changes in the stone-faced brunette who always sat in the aisle seat of the fourth pew. When the congregation was asked to pray she kept her head erect and her eyes open. During hymns she didn't pretend to sing or even bother opening the hymn book. It wasn't until her third visit to his office that Michael learned she worked in the Sheriff's Department and had access to all the files. In return for his guidance she offered hers.

"Of course I couldn't ask you to do anything illegal, Miss Garrison."

"Nor would I comply if you did," Miss Garrison said. "A little out of line perhaps but certainly within legal limits. You are the spiritual adviser to the child's family and as such you're entitled to know what has been done about the case so far. Doesn't that sound logical?"

"To me, yes. What about your boss?"

"My boss is like most bosses in other businesses. He has to depend on other people to tell him things, mainly me. Now and then there's something I neglect to tell him."

"And this is a now?"

"This is a now."

Miss Garrison provided a rough outline of what the files contained: the first report of the child's disappearance, lists of areas searched and names of searchers, interviews with the family, the neighbors, domestics, servicemen who regularly visited the neighborhood, gardeners, door-to-door salesmen, transients seen in the creek area, Annamay's teachers and friends at school, all the phone calls received, the hours spent, the miles covered, culminating in the discovery of the bones by an entomology student from the college on a beetle-collecting assignment, and finally in the pathologist's report.

It was a long file but as far as results were concerned it could have been condensed into a single sentence: Annamay Rebecca Hyatt had died of unknown causes, possibly asphyxiation, internal bleeding, shock, ruptured spleen, nobody knew.

"A lot of it is unimportant," Miss Garrison said. "Crank phone calls, letters offering theories and suggestions, searches that led nowhere, interviews with talkative people who had nothing to say, dumb questions and dumb answers. But I suppose you want it all."

"Every word of it, right from the beginning. Can you manage it?"

"You wouldn't have asked me if there'd been any doubt in your mind."

"I'd hate to get you into any trouble."

"I assure you," Miss Garrison said, "that I'd hate it even more. When do you want delivery to start?"

"Right away."

"It will have to be done in batches, of course. I can't monopolize the copying machine for any length of time. Although my co-workers are not likely to think I'm doing anything wrong, or even interesting, it's better not to invite questions."

"How will you get the material to me?"

Miss Garrison took off her steel-rimmed spectacles, as though she could see better without them. "I attend church regularly on Sundays and am treasurer of the ladies' auxiliary which meets every Wednesday night. I'm in the habit of carrying a large handbag, roomy enough to contain a couple of paperbacks and an extra sweater and rain gear, et cetera. In the past the size of my handbags has been the object of some speculation and humor around the office but now they are, like myself, taken for granted.

"Being taken for granted," Miss Garrison added, replacing her spectacles, "has certain advantages. I am part of the woodwork. No one expects woodwork to start acting like a tree again."

Howard's move into the guest cottage was accomplished quickly and without fuss. The cottage was always kept ready for occupancy, its cupboards and refrigerator well-stocked, even its medicine chest equipped with toothbrushes and paste, aspirin and throwaway razors. The only real change was the telephone which was now a private line with an unlisted number. Besides Michael, only two people were given this number—Kay, and Howard's confidential secretary.

During the move Howard's father stood around watching dolefully. He made no attempt to help Howard carry his personal effects over from the main house, and when asked to do so he refused with a sad little shake of his head.

"No, son, I cannot be a party to an act which I consider morally wrong."

"It surely isn't morally wrong to move from one section of my house to another."

"But what is the purpose of such an act?"

"I've already explained to you that I'm going to be very busy and I don't want to disturb Kay. . . . Here, hang this up for me, will you?"

The old man put his hands behind his back to prevent them from honoring the request without his approval. "You've always been very busy and Kay has never minded being disturbed. Throughout these many years she's been quite cheerfully keeping the hours necessary to people in the financial business like us, getting up at four-thirty so you could be at the office by six when the New York Stock Exchange opens."

"I don't want to argue with you, Dad, so I'll simply tell you for the last time that I'm going through with this project."

"Is this project so secret you can't even divulge it to me?"

"There's nothing to divulge yet. Perhaps there never will be. Now why don't you go work in the garden, Dad? Pick some mandarins. I noticed that one tree is loaded this year, dozens of them have fallen off."

"I picked ninety-three mandarins yesterday. Chizzy told me she didn't know what to do with ninety-three mandarins, and I wasn't to pick any more. You can't make pie or sauce out of them the way you can with apples, or juice them like oranges."

"Isn't it about time to prune the roses?"

"Ah, Howard, you've always been a good son to me. Don't start treating me like a foolish old fellow who must be kept busy. If you wish me not to bother you, you have only to say so in a clear direct manner. Would you prefer that I leave?"

"Yes."

"Then I will leave immediately. If you need me for anything I'll be up in the lighthouse logging ships."

"That's a good idea."

"No, it really isn't a good idea, Howard. You know it serves no purpose whatsoever, my keeping track of ships when no one ever reads my logs. If there's ever a war, of course, such logs might be of use, so perhaps I had better keep in practice."

The lighthouse was a thirty-foot tower built on the highest knoll on the property. It had a three-hundred-and-sixty-degree view of the sea, the coastline and the mountains behind the city that separated it from the rest of the world.

The tower contained a powerful telescope mounted on a tripod. Through it Mr. Hyatt could watch the stars by night and the ships by day. During the long dry season he kept the mountains under close observation for the first signs of a forest fire. During the wet season he often watched the freeway, the hundreds and thousands of cars and trucks and vans and campers driving north and south, all of them in a great hurry as if they feared the places they were going to wouldn't wait for them to get there.

He could also train the telescope on people but he seldom did because he considered spying an ungentlemanly pursuit. Only after Annamay disappeared did he use it for this purpose, scanning every part of the neighborhood that wasn't obscured by trees and hedges, fences and walls.

He was frequently astonished by what he saw. The maid next door, Ernestina, threw dishes into the garbage cans when she didn't feel like washing them. Her employers, who were traveling in Europe, were in for a shock when they came home, not merely at the reduction in their stock of dishes and cookware but also at the number of rats who'd developed a taste for Mexican food and lay hidden in the ivy and the crowns of palm trees awaiting their share.

The telescope also offered him a view farther on down the hill of the vine-covered pergola that connected the Cunninghams' house with the garage. Mrs. Cunningham could frequently be seen using this pergola. Her visits to the garage were quite puzzling since she didn't drive, and Mr. Hyatt reluctantly conceded that Chizzy had been right all along and Mrs. Cunningham had a great thirst.

Through the feathery leaves of a pepper tree, a section of the Cunninghams' pool area was also visible. Here Mrs. Cunningham's son, Peter, gave frequent pool parties which were unusual because the leaves of the pepper tree seemed to be all his guests ever wore. In contrast Mrs. Cunningham moved among the naked young men in her long billowy caftans and huge straw hats.

On a hill across the canyon was the Mediterranean villa of a mad old madam who kept a flock of white-coated attendants fluttering around her like trained doves. She came out on one of the balconies now and then to wave to the world.

Mr. Hyatt always waved back though he doubted that he could be seen.

Mr. Hyatt wasn't aware of her previous occupation until some time after she took over the villa. To him she appeared to be an ordinary elderly woman who dressed in long black robes rather like a nun's habit and employed a great many servants who didn't do much of anything except follow her around. In spite of the gardeners who came and went sporadically, the grounds were neglected. Fruit fell off trees and rotted, the oaks were alive with moths, the garden paths overgrown with devil grass. Mr. Hyatt brought the subject up one day when he and Chizzy were having lunch in the kitchen.

"I see we have a new neighbor."

"You *see*? How?"

"Through the telescope."

"That's all right then. Just so's you didn't go charging over to welcome her to the neighborhood. And if she ever approaches you take my advice and shun her like a rattlesnake."

"Why?"

"She is not," Chizzy said, "a woman of quality."

"She must be rich to have so many servants."

"Keepers, not servants. She came here from up north only one jump ahead of the cops and the butterfly nets."

"She may only be a trifle eccentric."

"She's mad as a hatter."

Mr. Hyatt swallowed this with a spoonful of soup. "Perhaps you would be interested in the origin of that phrase, mad as a hatter. In nineteenth-century England hatters did in fact go mad because the mercury compound they used to soften pelts affected their brains."

"Well, this old biddy didn't get that way by working on any hats, I can tell you."

"Of course not. The use of mercury was stopped some time ago."

"She is suffering," Chizzy said impatiently, "from an occupational disease. Now do you understand?"

"Dear me. Perhaps you should warn Annamay to keep away from there."

"You warn her. I've warned her about so many things it just goes in one ear and out the other."

Mr. Hyatt found Annamay in the palace bandaging Luella Lu who was somewhat the worse from another round of Shep's and Newf's toothy devotion. In the big house on the adjoining hill, Mr. Hyatt explained, lived a wicked witch who could cast evil spells on beautiful princesses, and must be avoided.

"I know," Annamay said. "Dru told me."

"Did she tell you the woman was a witch?"

"Sort of-ish." Dru's explanation had been rather unsettling since Annamay didn't understand what bad things people did to get bad diseases. She was grateful for her grandfather's reasonable alternative. Witches appeared in many of Annamay's storybooks, and while they were often fearsome they never got away with much in the long run.

The lure of having a spell cast on her proved irresistible. She persuaded Dru to accompany her. Leaving the dogs at home because they might attract attention by barking, the two girls ran through the avocado grove, jumped the creek and crept up the hill to the white stucco wall that surrounded the villa. Standing on Dru's shoulders Annamay peered into the courtyard. There was no witch in sight, only a young man in a white coat who was sitting reading a book.

He told her to get the hell out and she got the hell out.

"He's probably into dope," Dru said on the way back, "and suspects us of being narcs."

Dru's explanations had a life cycle of their own. Each one spawned a question which in turn had to hatch another explanation.

"What's a narc?"

"A narcotics investigator."

Annamay might have been flattered by this if Dru hadn't almost immediately added, "He doesn't know you're a child. All he saw of you was the top of your head and your eyes. Your eyes look a lot more grown-up and sensible than the rest of your face. It would have been a dead giveaway if he'd seen your teeth. Your teeth are positively childish."

"I don't care. I don't want to be suspected of being a narc anyway."

"I do."

"I don't."

"You," Dru said flatly, "are going to remain a child the rest of your life."

And she did. And the police came and went, and came again and left again throughout the summer, and toward the end of autumn the funeral was held. And Howard moved into the guest cottage, and Miss Esther Garrison made many trips between her files and the copying machine and went to church carrying her handbag. And the Reverend Michael Dunlop transferred its contents to his briefcase.

Chapter FIVE

The Reverend Michael Dunlop's wife, Lorna, saw the brief-case on the hall rack beside the front door.

She said, "Surely you're not going out again tonight."

"Yes."

"Why?"

"One of my parishioners wants to see me."

"What if your wife wants to see you too?"

"You're seeing me right now," Michael said, "and you're obviously not enjoying it much."

She had followed him out into the dimly lit hall of the house that went with the job in lieu of a decent salary. It was a mean little house with narrow windows that squeezed out the scenery. It had seemed cozy at first. The scenery didn't matter and Lorna's arms were loving. But the roof leaked in the winter rains and the place never had enough light even in summer and the upstairs room at the rear intended to be a nursery remained vacant.

"You don't give me much of a chance," Lorna said. "You've been acting so different lately, so secretive. We're married, we're supposed to share things, all kinds of things."

"Not everything can be shared, Lorna."

She pulled at a strand of her black curly hair as if she meant to straighten it out, straighten everything out. "Is this parishioner of yours a woman?"

"No."

"I guess that ought to reassure me. But it doesn't. You hear some awfully peculiar things these days about so-called respectable people."

"I'm not a bisexual if that's what you mean."

"I didn't mean—"

"You meant," Michael said. "Sorry I can't tell you the name of the man I'm going to see because if I did you'd want to know why and if I told you that I would be betraying a confidence."

She gave the strand of hair an extra-hard yank. "Oh, you're always so high-minded, aren't you? You can't understand how a lowbrow like me feels staying home alone every night with nothing to do but watch television."

"That's what you do when I stay home with you."

"No, it's not. We talk."

"Sure. We talk about what you're watching on television."

"If some of the married couples you counsel could see and hear us now they wouldn't believe you'd have nerve enough to be giving them advice on how to make a marriage work. No doubt it's more blessed to give than to receive when it's a matter of advice. It's certainly easier."

He smiled as he leaned down to kiss her. "Why, that's good, Lorna. Mind if I use it in one of my sermons?"

"Go ahead." She didn't return his smile or kiss but her face softened and he knew that the next day there would be a neatly typed note on his desk: File under ADVICE: It is more blessed to give than to receive, certainly easier.

"I'll make sure you get credit for it," Michael said.

"Oh, it's not that good." She picked up the gray-striped cat that was rubbing its back on her legs and held it against her left shoulder as if she were burping a baby. "Shall I wait up for you?"

"I'd rather you didn't, but you will anyway, I suppose."

"Yes."

"Is it me or is it Johnny Carson?"

"It will do you good to wonder," she said. "At least you're wearing your clerical collar. That gives you a protection of sorts."

In some neighborhoods like the Latino barrio it did. In others like the black ghetto it was more of a provocation at times, a reminder that God was white and right and rich. Since he was never sure where he was going he kept a change of clothes in the trunk of his car, well-worn jeans, a nylon jacket, a turtleneck sweater, sneakers and a black watch cap.

Among the materials Miss Garrison had copied and put in Michael's briefcase was a complete file of newspaper clippings covering a period of nearly four months.

Most of the clippings were from the local newspaper which ordinarily downplayed violent crimes but had assigned a full-time reporter to this one because of the prominence of the people involved and the overwhelming public interest in the little girl's disappearance. Everyone who had a child, knew a child or indeed had ever been a child, everyone in the city, county, state followed each step of the investigation.

It was discussed in bars and classrooms, at private clubs and public meetings.

Money was contributed to the original reward of fifty thousand dollars offered by the Hyatts. When the fund reached one hundred thousand Howard requested that it remain at that figure. If there was no legitimate claimant to the hundred thousand dollars, more dollars wouldn't make any difference and contributors' money could be put to better use elsewhere.

The ad appeared in every edition of the local paper. At first it had read:

HAVE YOU SEEN THIS CHILD?

Fifty thousand dollars reward for information leading to the return of Annamay Rebecca Hyatt, age eight.

There was a large picture of Annamay, the time and place
she was last seen and a complete description of her. Height,
four feet four, weight sixty-one pounds. Blue eyes, blond
straight shoulder-length hair, fair skin slightly sunburned,
mole on right wrist. Wearing faded blue denim shorts, blue
sandals, striped T-shirt stamped with her initials, ARH.

After the bones were found the entire wording of the ad
was altered.

ONE HUNDRED THOUSAND DOLLARS REWARD FOR IN-
FORMATION LEADING TO THE ARREST AND ARRAIGN-
MENT OF THE PERSON OR PERSONS RESPONSIBLE FOR
THE DEATH OF ANNAMAY REBECCA HYATT.

The local television station also carried four sixty-second
spots of the offer every twenty-four hours. These included a
close-up of the child and a short segment of a movie Kay
had taken of Annamay with the two dogs.

The ads failed to bring forward anyone with a reasonable
claim or even a plausible story, but the police dutifully made
a report of each one. Howard and Michael read them all
through at their first meeting in the guest cottage.

Mrs. Edwina Pascal, thirty-two, of 2003 Estero Gordo
Street, Santa Felicia, claimed that her husband, Geronimo'
had molested their daughter and his stepdaughter, had
probably done the same thing to the Hyatt girl and should
be put in the gas chamber.

Truman Wilson, forty-five, no fixed address, charged that
his best friend had disappeared on the same day that Annamay did and he was positive there was a connection. The
friend owed him ninety-three dollars and was no damn
good. Wilson planned to use the reward money to buy a
racehorse but he couldn't remember his friend's last name,
and the money remained in the bank.

A female psychic offered to pay her own fare from Connecticut if she would be allowed to stay in the princess's palace for a week to absorb the atmosphere and possibly establish contact with Annamay's spirit. The reward money would be used not for her personal gain but to found a center for the study of parapsychology. Her letter included a phone number.

Howard got in touch with her.

"I was like a terminally ill cancer patient reaching for laetrile," he told Michael. "So I called her."

"What did she say?"

"Nothing. She was too stoned to talk."

Small blond girls sprang up like mushrooms all over town: alone, with a young man, an old man, a black man and woman, three teenagers, and an entire Mexican family. One of the reports came from a Mrs. Jeanette Orchard who claimed she saw a middle-aged man at a gas station with a blond child who was crying. A follow-up by a sheriff's deputy revealed that the middle-aged man owned the gas station and the child, a short fat ten-year-old, was crying because he wouldn't let her have any more candy bars. Mrs. Orchard was extremely disappointed since she'd put a down payment on a mobile home in anticipation of the reward money.

"At least she didn't want to buy a racehorse," Howard said, laying aside the reward file. "What's next?"

"Pictures," Michael said. "Hundreds, from publications throughout the country. There's not much point in looking at all of them."

"I think there is. We decided in the beginning that we'd examine all the police files in the hope of finding an area they failed to cover. Wasn't that our mutual decision?"

"Yes."

"So, let's go."

There were literally hundreds, carefully labeled, each subject identified and each photographer credited, with the date and place taken and the initials of the deputy who had filed the picture.

There were formal poses of Annamay intended for Christmas gifts, and snapshots of her at play and at school; of the school itself; of the house Annamay lived in and the palace and even of the man who'd designed them both, Benjamin York. There were pictures of Kay and Howard together and separately; of Chizzy coming out of the coroner's inquest; Dru in the hall of the courthouse standing between her mother and stepfather, looking small and scared. Even Mitsu and Suki, who normally smiled a great deal, stared somberly into the camera as if it were a judge.

There were also pictures of nearly everyone who lived, worked, or visited in the neighborhood, from Ernestina, the maid next door to the Hyatts, caught throwing a plate into the garbage can, to the old madam waving to the world from one of the balconies of her villa. The madam lent a sinister air to the case as bits and pieces of her past came out in the newspaper accounts.

It was hinted in one of these accounts that the madam had supplied children to some of her special customers, but a disclaimer was printed in the next edition. Many people missed seeing the disclaimer and others regarded it simply as a ploy to avoid a possible libel suit. The madam received crank letters she wasn't allowed to read and crank phone calls that weren't relayed to her. The upshot of the matter was that her conservators found it expedient to double the wages of her household staff.

All the members of the staff had been interviewed by sheriff's deputies, some briefly, some at length, depending on the verbosity of both parties involved. But the madam herself had not been questioned.

The file listed her real name as Rosa Firenze. Born in Chicago, raised in a succession of foster homes until her first arrest at age thirteen for aggravated assault. After a series of arrests she drifted westward and finally discovered her destiny. In San Francisco at the beginning of World War II Rosa found the fleet and the fleet found her.

Michael said, "Why wasn't Miss Firenze questioned?"

"Since she has been declared incompetent by the court her lawyer's permission was necessary and he refused to give it. So officially the police could do nothing."

"And unofficially?"

"Miss Firenze sometimes escapes from the grounds. On one of these occasions a deputy found her wandering around the neighborhood and exchanged words with her. The exchange didn't last very long. An attendant arrived and whisked her away. But according to my informant she was coherent and eager to talk to an outsider. There is even a rumor," Howard added, "that she is writing her memoirs and the whole crazy lady bit is a ploy to keep her under observation. There are undoubtedly a certain number of bigwigs in the armed services and politics who would prefer to keep Miss Firenze out of print and circulation. I'm inclined to doubt the memoirs story. She's the kind of woman who inspires such stories, maybe starts a few of them herself."

"If the rumor is true," Michael said, "Miss Firenze might be interested in seeing a publisher."

"You."

"Me."

"You could be pretty convincing, I'm sure. But if the rumor is false you blow your chance of ever seeing her. Better stick to your own profession."

"What makes you think she might want to see a minister?"

"I have a hunch. My dad, who's spotted her through the telescope in the lighthouse, says she wears clothes that look like a nun's habit. That could indicate some sort of penitence on her part."

"Maybe. I'll give it a try anyway."

Rosa Firenze's name was added to the list of subjects needing further attention. More interviews were read aloud, first by one man, then by the other, until it was almost midnight and they were both tired, and Howard was depressed as well. Although more than a dozen names were added to the list, no really promising leads emerged from the mass of material, no glaring omissions on the part of the police.

What had started out as a serious project with a chance of succeeding now seemed hardly more than a child's game Annamay and Dru might have played after finding one of the goldfish dead in the lily pond or coming across the body of a bird or butterfly. Throughout the gardens the graves of many small creatures were marked by miniature crosses made of twigs or popsicle sticks. *We are two grown men playing with twigs,* Howard thought.

He sat by the window which had a view of the main house. His father's quarters were dark, but lights were still on in the kitchen and Chizzy's room downstairs and in Kay's bedroom upstairs. He was surprised at how little time it had taken him to think of it as Kay's bedroom although the closets and drawers still contained most of his clothes.

He opened the window. The smells of autumn drifted in, damp earth, eucalyptus wood burning in someone's fireplace, lemon blossoms. But the most teasing and pervasive of all was the scent of bread baking. Chizzy was cooking again to bake away her blues. And while Chizzy cooked, he and Michael were playing a child's game for the same reason.

"What if we're only wasting our time?" Howard said. "We can't bring her back anyway."

"No, but we might prevent another child from suffering the same fate."

"Face it, Mike. We're dreamers, that's all. Dreamers."

"Okay, so I'm a dreamer," Michael said. "Wake me when the world is over."

"I wish I had your kind of faith."

"And what kind is that?"

"Whatever it is that keeps you going."

"What would keep me going right now is a slice of Chizzy's homemade bread. Let's go over and beg some from her."

"Good idea."

Chizzy was flustered by the sudden appearance of company. She pulled her plaid flannel robe around her and tried to tidy her wiry gray hair. Neither effort was successful. She had long since outgrown the robe and her hair always looked the same, resisting her determined attacks on it with brush and comb. It sat on her head like a steel-wool scouring pad.

"I didn't mean to wake anybody," she said, wiping her hands on the dish towel that dangled from one pocket of her robe. "I was waiting for Miss Kay to come home and I decided to pass the time by doing a bit of baking."

The bit of baking filled one entire section of the counter. There were at least a dozen loaves of various shapes and sizes, including a very tiny one which Chizzy attempted to hide before either of her unexpected guests saw it. Howard saw it anyway and knew the miniature loaf had been made for Annamay. He averted his eyes and Chizzy finished her clumsy job of hiding it in the cupboard.

"I was about to wrap everything and pop it in the freezer. I don't suppose you'd like a slice or two."

"You suppose wrong," Michael said. "That's why we're here."

The two men sat down at the kitchen table while Chizzy sliced the bread and brought out butter and jam and put milk on the stove to heat for chocolate.

Howard said, "What time did she get home?"

"About fifteen minutes ago."

"I didn't hear Ben's car."

"She came in a taxi," Chizzy said. "Which in my opinion was the rightful thing to do under the circumstances."

"What circumstances?"

"Married women should not be seen at this time of night with younger men in sports cars."

"Ben took her to a concert. I asked him to."

But the explanation didn't satisfy Chizzy's hunger for reassurance. She added twice as much cocoa and sugar to the milk as she should have, so there was enough hot chocolate for half a dozen people. Whatever was left over she would of course finish herself, and the flannel robe would become tighter and her self-image more distorted, a thin woman followed by a fat shadow.

"Won't you join us?" Howard said.

"No, thanks, I'm not hungry." This was certainly true since she had eaten the first loaf that came out of the oven in order to test its quality and half the next loaf as well to make sure it conformed. "All this aggravation has disturbed my appetite. And I bet there's someone sitting in this very room who's just as aggravated as I am."

She glanced pointedly at Michael who responded with a shrug. "Aggravation has never disturbed my appetite, especially if I don't know what I'm supposed to be aggravated about."

"Things aren't normal around here," Chizzy said. "They're not *normal*."

"Normal changes from day to day, Chizzy."

"Why?"

"Because events happen. Circumstances change and so people change. The world is always in a state of flux."

Bulloney, Chizzy thought, but she didn't say it out loud. Although she had no religion herself, so many people did that she was forced to concede the possibility that there was Somebody Up There listening and she didn't want to be heard talking back to a minister. It seemed only fair, however, that she be allowed to disagree politely.

"I don't buy that flux business, begging your Reverend's pardon. No sir. Everything around this place went along the same, year after year. *That* was normal."

74

"And you want it back."

"Oh, I know I can't have it all back. But Miss Kay and Mr. Howard, I could have them."

"You're talking about me as if I'd gone away," Howard told her. "I didn't. I'm still here."

"Not to me you aren't, not like in the old days. All I've got now is the old man and the two dogs and a bunch of silly-looking fish."

"Don't let my father hear you call them that. He paid twenty thousand dollars for the big black one."

"He got taken, if you ask me."

"My father's not easy to take. I learned that before I entered school. The black fish is a magoi, eighty-three years old. You know that, Chizzy."

"I've been told. That doesn't make it the truth."

"The magoi belonged to the same Japanese family for three generations. These koi have pedigrees much like dogs."

"Well, give me an eighty-three-year-old dog any day."

"This," Michael said glancing at his watch, "is definitely not normal. I'm sitting at midnight eating hot homemade bread and discussing an eighty-three-year-old fish. Flux, Chizzy, flux."

"What's so great about getting old anyway? It's not as if we become more valuable like koi. I certainly don't want to live to be eighty-three."

"Don't worry, you won't," Howard said, "unless you lose some of that blubber."

"I have a glandular disorder," Chizzy said coldly. "You paid for me to go to that diet doctor and that's what he told me."

"Is it?"

"Well, if you can believe that damn fish is eighty-three years old you can believe I have a glandular disorder."

"I think it's time for me to leave," Michael said, and no one gave him any argument. Chizzy was prepared to defend her glandular disorder to the death and Howard was unlikely to subtract even a year from the age of the fish. "Thanks for the snack, Chizzy."

"Just a minute. I'll give you some to take home."

She put four loaves in a large paper sack and followed him outside. By the time they reached his car, an old Buick bequeathed to him by a member of his congregation, Chizzy was puffing as if she'd been carrying bricks. He put the bag in the trunk of the Buick and waited a minute or two until Chizzy caught her breath.

"You really ought to lose some weight, Chizzy. Exactly what did the doctor tell you?"

"That I eat too much. Imagine getting paid for telling fat people they eat too much. What a racket."

"No glandular disorder?"

"No. But I can't admit that to Mr. Howard. I wouldn't want him to think he had wasted his money."

"That's very considerate of you," Michael said gravely.

"Also I'd hate him to think I was just a pig. Because I wouldn't be if things were normal again."

"They'll never be the same again. But they'll be normal because your concept of normal will change."

"Highfalutin words like concept and flux don't mean a hoot to me. What's right is right."

"You're a hard case, Chizzy. Good night. And thanks for the bread."

Howard went upstairs and knocked on the door of what had recently been his own room.

"Kay?"

"Come in."

She was standing by the window still wearing her concert clothes, a long-skirted, royal-blue velvet suit with fake diamond buttons that looked exactly like the real diamonds she wore in her ears. He had given her the earrings as a wedding present before he found out she didn't much like jewelry of any kind. Tonight she was not only wearing the earrings, she was drawing attention to them by having her hair pulled back severely into a French knot.

He noticed that there were a few strands of gray in her hair. He still thought of her as a girl and the gray hairs disturbed him, made him feel that he had turned away for a few minutes and looked back to find that years had passed.

He said, "Did you have a good time?"

"Yes."

There was a long silence.

"Is that all, yes?"

"Do you want a blow-by-blow description? All right. Ben picked me up at seven-thirty. We arrived at the theater early so we had some wine in the lounge. Chablis, I think. I wasn't paying much attention to the wine because I could feel people staring at me. They probably thought I should be at home crying. Then that dreadful woman from down the road, Mrs. Cunningham, came up and started a conversation. I guess it was a conversation. I could hardly understand what she was saying. She kept talking about a meat loaf, and how she was allergic to meat loaf and that's why she couldn't accept it. She babbled on while that son of hers stood there not saying a word, smiling that nasty little smile of his. The music was fine though I can't remember what it was. I kept thinking of that damn meat loaf. Do you know anything about a meat loaf?"

"I could write a book about meat loaf," Howard said. "Meat loaf prep school, meat loaf college cafeteria, fraternity, country club, Mother's, Chizzy's—"

"Chizzy," Kay repeated. "That's it. Chizzy got into one of her cooking fits and started distributing food around the neighborhood again. You must talk to her about that, Howard."

"I'd rather she distribute it than eat it.... You look nice tonight, Kay. Is that a new outfit?"

"Yes."

"Pretty color. Did you have supper after the concert?"

"No. Was I supposed to?"

"Chizzy said you missed dinner. You must be hungry."

"Sorry, Howard. If you programmed me to be hungry, better check your computer. I'm not." She removed her earrings as if they'd suddenly begun to pinch. "Do you want the rest of the report on Kay's big night out? Well, Ben invited me to go dancing at a supper club and I refused. I didn't feel like dancing and I didn't want any more music. Or any more Ben either, for that matter. He was trying so hard to make me enjoy myself that he made me nervous. I came home alone in a taxi. If Ben wants to go dancing let him take his Ms. Quinn."

"No one can please you anymore, Kay."

"Then why doesn't everybody simply stop trying?"

"Because we love you."

"I don't want to be loved. I want to be let alone."

"All right. Good night, Kay."

"Good night."

He went out, closing the door quietly behind him. He had turned away for a few minutes and when he looked back again there was gray in Kay's hair and she didn't want anyone to love her.

He was halfway down the steps when Kay's door opened again and she came to the head of the staircase.

"By the way," she said in a cool dry voice, "next time you buy tickets for a concert, please remember that I prefer to sit a little farther back."

"I didn't buy the tickets."

"They were waiting at the box office in your name."

"Ben paid for them. My secretary merely made the reservations."

"How sweet. I suppose she loves me too."

"Most secretaries consider the boss's wife a pain in the

neck," Howard said. "I don't imagine mine is any exception."

"Hurray. There's nothing more bracing than a dose of good honest hate. It's like a spring tonic."

Another long silence fell over them like a mist net used to trap birds.

"Will you be going out with Ben another time, Kay?"

"If that's what you have me programmed for. There's probably a computer readout on your secretary's desk right now with everything arranged but the weather. Maybe you could even do something about that too. I wouldn't put it past you to try."

"Why all this hostility, Kay?"

"Those people who stared at me at the concert tonight," she said bitterly, "they were right. I should have been home crying."

Shelley Quinn's centerfold body was hidden under a pair of Ben's pajamas and crumpled into his favorite lounge chair. Quinn was simultaneously eating an apple and combing her long auburn hair, still damp from a shampoo.

Ben noted that she didn't appear particularly happy at his return. She looked at him over the top of a pair of horn-rimmed spectacles he had never seen before. It was a solemn look, as if he had interrupted something very important.

She said, "Hi," and put down the comb and the apple and turned off the radio. "All I could find to eat around here was an apple. Don't you ever buy any groceries?"

"Not if I can help it."

"And another thing, why do you live in a dump like this?"

"I like dumps."

"I mean it, Benjie. You should build yourself a showplace, put up more of a front."

"I like your front."

"Be serious. Why do you want to live like this?"

"It suits me," Ben said.

"I don't see how it can suit you, listening to people walking around upstairs and the television blaring next door and cars coming and going all night."

He didn't try to explain that these were the very things that gave him privacy, more privacy than Howard had on his exclusive eight acres. Everyone knew where and how Howard lived. Nobody knew much about the tenant in the front apartment of the Vista del Mar, and nobody cared. The old apartment house was squeezed between a cluster of expensive oceanfront condos on one side and commercial development on the other. Both sides were fighting to tear it down and turn it into a parking lot. Meanwhile the card on the front mailbox was printed York, and underneath it the name Quinn written in green ink which was Quinn's favorite color. Both names looked impermanent. A hundred had preceded them; perhaps a hundred would come later.

Ben went into the bedroom to hang up his jacket. Quinn's clothes were strewn around the room as though she'd had some old school friends in for a slumber party. "This place is a mess."

"I know. I'm collecting my laundry to take over to Mom's. Moms are really great, aren't they?"

"I don't know. I never had any."

"Well, don't feel bad. Sometimes they're not so great. Would you like a drink, Benjie?"

"I would."

"Me too. I'll take a spritzer."

"I thought you were offering to make me a drink."

"No, I wasn't. You're always telling me to be precise, so I was. But what's the use of me speaking precise if you don't listen precise? All I said was—"

"Okay, okay, I make the drinks."

"Good. I'm too tired. I've been working like a dog all evening."

"Doing what, vandalizing my bedroom?"

"I was doing," Quinn said, frowning, "exactly what you told me to. You said if I wanted to improve myself I should listen to discussion programs and make notes, write down words I didn't know and stuff like that. So I did." From the table beside her she picked up a notebook. "It was a real interesting discussion, all about sexual abrasions."

"And what are sexual abrasions?"

"You know, kinky stuff."

"The word is aberrations," he said, and spelled it for her.

"It sure sounded like abrasions to me. Anyway, I was surprised to find out how innocent I am, considering. Listen to this one. A-i-l-u-r-o-p-h-i-l-e. Know what that means?"

"No."

"It means a guy who gets turned on by cats. How's that for a sickie?"

He handed her a glass of white wine. "Here's your spritzer, minus the club soda we don't have and the lemon we also don't have."

"Gosh, Benjie, you really should buy some groceries."

"I will, any day now."

"You probably have a lousy diet."

"Probably."

She took a sip of the wine, then returned to her notebook. "Here's another dandy. P-e-d-o-p-h-i-l-e. I know what it means but I didn't know there was a word for it. Did you?"

Ben didn't answer.

"I asked you a question, Benjie. Did you know there was a word for a guy who gets turned on by little children?"

"Shut up."

"Hey, you can't talk to me like that; we're not married. Here I spend a whole evening doing what you told me to and all you have to say is shut up."

"That's all I have to say—shut up."

As if she were getting ready to slug it out, Quinn removed her spectacles and put the notebook back on the table. But by the time she unfolded herself from the chair Ben had disappeared into the kitchen. She followed him.

He was standing in front of the sink which had the only view window of the apartment. The night was clear and moonless. Strings of lights lined the breakwater and the marina walkways. There were lights also in the harbormaster's office and the all-night café underneath it, and in a few of the live-aboard boats.

No matter what the weather, this window was kept open so that Ben could hear, during lulls in the traffic along the oceanfront boulevard, the waves smashing against the breakwater. The sound of this incessant attack excited him. It was the sound of war and there was no doubt who the winner would be. The concrete of the breakwater was already crumbling in spots and its exposed reinforcing cables and iron railings were rusting.

"Benjie?"

Quinn knew how he hated to be touched when he was upset, so she stood behind him within touching distance and said again softly, "Benjie? Listen, I'm sorry. I forgot all about the little Hyatt girl when I said that word. Is there anything I can do to make it up to you?"

"Yes. You can finish packing your laundry and take it over to your mother's and stay there."

"I can't believe you're serious, Benjie."

"Force yourself."

"It's not reasonable. Why should one mistake, in fact why should a little girl I've never even seen come between me and a guy I really like? I really *like* you, Benjie. We suit each other, we fit, we're exactly the right size for each other. You can't imagine how awkward it is sometimes when you get a really big guy—"

"I'll try."

"I mean, you and me, we fit together so great I could drop off to sleep while we're, you know, together, except I always have to go potty afterward."

"Will you for God's sake stop using expressions like go potty? You're a grown woman."

"My mom still says it and she's nearly fifty. She taught me never to use obscene language and I never ever do. Kindly remember that I didn't *say* those words I heard on the discussion program, I *spelled* them."

"I see. It's all right to spell them."

"It's not really all right, it's just not quite so wrong.... This woman you took to the concert tonight because her husband was busy, is she as old as my mom?"

"No."

"Well?"

"What do you mean, well?"

"Well, don't you want to tell me how old she is?"

"I don't want to and I'm not going to."

"Is she pretty?"

"Yes."

"As pretty as I am?"

"Yes."

"But she's a lot older."

"She's a lot smarter," Ben said. "Too smart to ask the kind of questions you've been asking."

"If she's a friend of the family like you claim, I don't see why you should be so secretive about her. Anyway, you told me you never had a mother so how can you have a family? I think you're lying to me, Benjie, and lying is wrongful like bad language."

"Right now I feel like doing something more wrongful than either of them." He turned and grabbed her by the shoulder. "So I suggest you get the h-e-l-l out of here before I knock the s-h-i-t out of you."

"Who are you trying to scare anyway? I don't scare that easy. Another one of the things my mom taught me is how to knee a guy in exactly the right place."

"Your mother must be a mine of information."

"You're d-a-m tootin she is."

Shrugging off his hand she walked back into the living room and rearranged herself in the lounge chair and turned the radio on again. The program had changed. A man was discussing musical terms and it wasn't nearly as interesting so she went to bed.

After a while Benjie came to bed too, and Quinn, who was a kindhearted girl, welcomed him. She still didn't understand why he had reacted so violently and she decided she would ask her mother when she took the laundry over. Because her mother liked to set a good example to her offspring by spelling out certain words, it probably would be a long conversation.

One thing was for sure: Benjie was no p-e-d-o-p-h-i-l-e.

Chapter SIX

That night Michael Dunlop lay awake for a long time planning how and when he should approach Miss Firenze in her villa. He finally decided on early morning because in his rather wide experience with disturbed people he'd found this was when they were most rational and alert.

But in the morning the old Buick wouldn't start. Lorna said he knew nothing about cars (true), that he'd forgotten to have the oil changed (probably true), and that she could and would start it herself (not true). When the tow truck finally arrived he hitched a ride with the driver as far as Howard's house.

Howard, who always went to the office at six, had been gone for hours but Kay was backing her station wagon out of the garage with Chizzy in the front seat and the two dogs in the back.

All four looked happy to see him, although only the German shepherd indicated it vocally.

"What are you doing here?" Kay said when Shep's greeting had subsided.

"I thought I'd take a walk."

"A walk? Where?"

"Oh, through your avocado grove."

"Well, make sure your shoes aren't carrying root rot," Chizzy said.

Michael glanced at his shoes. They didn't appear to have any root rot, whatever that was. "I'm clean."

"Where did you leave your car?" Kay asked him.

"At the garage."

"And you came all the way over here to walk through our avocado grove?"

"Yes."

"Why?"

"A number of reasons."

"I told you," Chizzy said to Kay. "Didn't I tell you? He and Mr. Howard are playing detective. Like a couple of kids who've been watching too much television. It wasn't hard to figure out, what with them staying up till all hours and having a secret telephone installed."

"It's not a secret telephone," Michael said. "It has an unlisted number, that's all."

"Same difference."

Kay was watching him somberly. "Why are you wearing your collar?"

"I thought it might be useful."

"For walking through an avocado grove?"

"That too."

"You don't intend to answer any of my questions, do you?"

"I'd rather not."

"It's a sneaky business, if you ask me," Chizzy said.

"Nobody asked you," Kay told her, and turned back to Michael. "Whatever you and Howard are up to, please be careful."

"There's no danger."

"I don't want anything to happen to either of you."

"There's no danger," Michael repeated.

It had never even occurred to him that there could be. He was merely going to visit a crazy old lady.

* * *

The villa was surrounded by a white stucco wall and its entrance guarded by an eight-foot iron-grillwork gate. On one side of the gate there was a voice box connected to the main house but Michael saw little point in trying to use it. No human voice could have been heard over the noise of the gasoline-powered blower being operated by one of the gardeners. He wore the gas tank on his back like a hump, a strange new mutation in a strange new world of splitting atoms and eardrums.

The blower was scattering leaves and dirt from one side of the driveway to the other and back again. The operator, wearing earphones to protect his hearing, seemed to be enjoying the game. He looked disappointed when he had to acknowledge Michael's presence, turn off the motor and remove his earphones.

"Good morning," Michael said.

The man's perfunctory nod indicated that this might or might not be true.

"I'd like to see Miss Firenze."

"She don't see a whole bunch of people but you can try if you want. Press the button on the voice box and wait for someone to answer, then tell them who you are and what you're after. I see you're a man of the cloth."

"Yes."

"First one to come here that I can recall. Is the old lady dying?"

"Not to my knowledge."

"Must be close to it. Ninety if she's a day."

"Seventy-three."

"She'd had more than ninety years of experience judging from the stories I hear."

Michael pressed the button on the gate and when there was no response pressed it again. Another half minute passed before a woman's voice said brusquely, "Ms. Leigh here. Who's there?"

"I am the Reverend Michael Dunlop."

"The *who*?"

"The Reverend Michael Dunlop. I'd like to see Miss Firenze if I may."

"Is this some kind of gag?"

"No. Every month or so I try to get around to making a few community calls on people whose names are presented to me."

"Well, whoever presented Firenze's name must have a weird sense of humor. Anyway she's still in bed eating her breakfast. Do you reverend people pay social calls on ladies in bed?"

"Frequently. I make regular hospital rounds."

"She's not sick. She simply stays in her room a lot because that's where we work. I'm her ghost-writer, collaborator, amanuensis, you name it."

"It sounds like interesting work," Michael said. "I'd like to hear about it."

"I don't buy that. But it's been a dull week so come on in."

The gate opened almost immediately and Michael went inside. When he heard the gate close behind him he suffered the same feeling he always had when he visited the jail, that the electrical system would fail some day and he would be trapped inside, a prisoner no better than the others.

Walking up the driveway he passed two gardeners clipping a privet hedge, an Oasis Pool Service truck and a white-coated attendant carrying a stack of magazines. No greetings were exchanged. The power blower had started up again, monopolizing the air like the manic roar of a new world tyrant.

The intricately carved front door was opened by Ms. Leigh herself, a tall young Chinese woman with short geometrically cut black hair. She wore steel-rimmed glasses and a green-plaid skirt and green sweater with white collar and cuffs. She looked so efficient that Michael suspected she wasn't.

She proved it immediately. "What did you say your name was?"

"Is. It was Michael Dunlop when you asked me before and it still is."

Ms. Leigh looked slightly annoyed. "Oh, you're one of those grammar freaks, are you? You'll have a field day with Firenze. It's *my* job to correct *her* grammar."

"Am I going to be permitted to see her?"

"Why not? She perked up when I told her there was a minister here for a visit. Maybe she's all ready to be converted, but don't bet the rent on it. She's having, by the way, a lucid day. Which is to say she's not as nutty as she was yesterday." Ms. Leigh looked him up and down carefully before she closed the door. "I presume you're aware she's not playing with a full deck."

"Yes, but I'm not sure how many cards are missing."

"It varies from moon to moon. Also from man to man. You may get lucky." Not a mucle moved on Ms. Leigh's smooth impassive face but she seemed to be amused. "Depending on your idea of luck and what's on your mind."

The hall was almost as large as a ballroom. Its polished tile floor reflected the lights of two crystal chandeliers. Along one wall was a trio of pink velvet chairs that looked as if they had come from Miss Firenze's past and their gold-braid trim belonged on some officer's uniform. The rest of the furniture was in the Spanish tradition of old Santa Felicia, dark wood and stiff-backed benches and chairs that made no concessions to the human frame.

The floor was so slippery Michael could hardly walk on it. This explained Ms. Leigh's jogging shoes and the peculiar gait of the maid who was carrying a breakfast tray down the hall.

"We'd better give Firenze a few minutes to primp," Ms.

89

Leigh said. "There's a nice little solarium off the library. It's the only cheerful room in the place so I often use it as an office. . . . Do you like plants?"

"Should I?"

"I see we understand each other," Ms. Leigh said. "Yes, you should. They're Firenze's hobby. What's your favorite?"

"Roses."

"Firenze hates roses. She says they're too much like women, always demanding to be admired and then turning around and scratching you when you come near them."

"Miss Firenze evidently doesn't think much of women."

"No. Odd, isn't it? Or perhaps not so odd. She doesn't think much of men either."

The solarium was a glass-walled room filled with plants of various sizes and shapes in all kinds of containers. The tile floor slanted down to a drain in the center of the room and the air was heavy with moisture. The only furniture was a desk in one corner and two white wicker settees with yellow vinyl cushions.

Ms. Leigh examined the underside of a red-leafed plant, then pulled a leaf off and showed it to Michael. "Notice that fine webbing? You can't see the nasty little beast responsible for it but he's there all right, and so are all his relatives. Red spider mites. Hard to get rid of. Sit down."

Michael sat down on one of the wicker settees. It crackled and creaked in protest under his weight. "I'd like to hear about your job, Ms. Leigh."

"Why?"

"I've never met a ghost-writer before."

"Actually I'm not a ghost-writer, I'm a real writer. At least I think I am. Anyway, I'm only ghosting until my husband gets a break in Hollywood. He's an actor."

"Meanwhile, what do you do for Miss Firenze?"

"Listen. Change tapes. Transcribe what's transcribable. Sometimes it's fairly sensible and interesting. Other times it's profanity or gibberish and I have to clean it up or make sense out of it or ignore it. I do a lot of ignoring."

"Then the rumor is true, that she's writing her memoirs?"

"They can't really be called memoirs because she gets mixed up about names and dates and places. But I suppose it all happened one way or another at one time or another. Her language is often quite picturesque, probably because she's not inhibited by rules of grammar or by common sense or discipline of any kind. None of it will ever be published, of course, but as long as she keeps talking, Larry and I keep eating and paying for his drama lessons. The money isn't the only reason I'm staying, though. Her book will never be published but maybe mine will."

"And what's yours?"

"Mine will be a book about trying to write her book. It could be quite funny. I've kept notes on some of the things she does and says, so I have plenty of material. I also have a title. *Madam.* Oh, I know *Madam* has been used in dozens of titles, *Madame Bovary, Madame X,* and so on. But this is different, don't you think? I mean, it's provocative. Isn't it?"

"I find the whole idea provocative."

"You do? Really?"

"Yes indeed," Michael said. "You have a day-to-day chronicle on what's happened around the villa?"

"Chronicle is too big a word. It's a collection of haphazard notes, some of her reminiscences, her fits and foibles."

"What causes her fits?"

"Practically everything, even the weather. Fog is a good example. It depresses her so badly she shuts herself up in her room and mopes for hours. That leaves the staff with considerable time to kill. The attendants read or play cards or watch television. I work on the diary. I can't simply go home because she might snap out of it at any minute if the fog lifts. She equates fog," Ms. Leigh explained, "with ectoplasm, the spirit world trying to get in touch with her, ghoulies and ghosties and things that go bump in the night.

San Francisco was her place of business so I'm sure there was a lot of fog in her life. Also a lot of things that went bump in the night."

Michael had another opportunity to admire the way Ms. Leigh could look amused without moving a single facial muscle. "How do other kinds of weather affect her?"

"Fortunately we don't have much thunder and lightning around here because that's what really drives her batty. The santanas do too, these dry dirty winds that blow in from the desert. She's scared to death of them. She tears around the house closing all the windows and drapes and screaming that they're out to get her."

"Who are 'they'?"

"I wish I knew. I'd invite them in and say, take her, she's yours. Mostly though, it's not a bad job. We even get a little excitement now and then when Firenze escapes. We usually let her stay out for an hour or so and have her fun, then send someone after her. It's a change for all of us."

"Where does she go when she escapes?"

"Down to the creek. She plays in the water like a kid and brings back little bouquets of flowers, or what she pretends are flowers. Sometimes, it's only a handful of grass or foxtails, once even poison oak. We all thought she'd be a real mess afterward but she fooled us again. It turned out that she's immune to it. There wasn't a blister or red mark on her. She could probably make a salad of the stuff and it wouldn't do her any harm."

The young maid Michael had seen carrying the breakfast tray down the hall appeared in the doorway. "Madam just buzzed that she's ready."

"Thanks, Miriam. We'll go right up."

Miss Firenze was propped up on half a dozen pillows in the center of a king-sized bed. Her body was completely hidden under a black garment that resembled the robes worn by members of a church choir.

92

Age had left her skin relatively unlined but rearranged the hair on her face. She had no eyebrows or lashes, but a profusion of gray-black hairs grew out of her upper lip almost as thick as a moustache. Under it she wore a slash of bright red lipstick. Her still-black hair was arranged in a single braid at the back of her neck. Her eyes were her most striking feature, as bright and iridescent as drops of oil.

She addressed her visitor in a voice that was hoarse, as if her vocal chords had lost their elasticity from overuse.

"So what have we here?"

"I'm Michael Dunlop, Miss Firenze."

"Don't mean a thing to me. Wait. That's thirteen letters. Bad luck. You're bringing me bad luck."

"I don't think so."

"What's your sign?"

"Sign?"

"When were you born?"

"December thirteenth."

"Thirteen again. Two thirteens. I don't like this. Take him away. He's bad luck."

"Madam is forgetting," Ms. Leigh said smoothly, "that two thirteens make twenty-six and twenty-six is a good round lucky number."

"Who says so?"

"Your book on numerology."

"It says right there in print that twenty-six is lucky?"

"Right there in print."

Miss Firenze's bright gaze shifted back to Michael. "Come on over here where I can get a look at you. Stand by the window."

Michael stood by the window. It had iron grillwork across it like the iron grilling on the front gate. He was not sure whether it was intended to keep people out or to keep Miss Firenze in.

"You're not a bad-looking fellow. A bit too skinny. A

man should be on the heavy side, robust, strong. You like flowers?"

"Yes."

"What's your favorite?"

"Carnations," Ms. Leigh said. "He told me on the way up here how much he admires carnations."

"Now ain't that a coincidence? Carnations are my favorite too. Nice spicy smell, not too sweet like jasmine or roses. You like roses?"

"Not particularly," Michael said.

"Good. Sit down."

Michael sat down in a pink velvet chair that matched the trio he'd seen in the hall. As Miss Firenze watched him the skin around her eyes crinkled and the slash of lipstick under her moustache moved in what appeared to be a smile. It was more mischievous than friendly, as if she were recalling someone else who'd sat in that chair, or a long succession of someone elses.

"So. You're a minister."

"Yes."

"What's that thing you're wearing?"

"A clerical collar."

"No, no, no. I mean the black thing that looks like a vest on backwards."

"It's called a rabat."

"I've often wondered about that. I've seen quite a few of them in my day. You fellows don't always practice what you preach, you know. But then who does? I remember telling my girls to always brush their teeth three times a day, and all the time I was only brushing mine twice a day. I should have listened to myself. Oh, I still got all my teeth, yes sir, but they're in a cigar box along with my gallstones and wedding ring."

From Ms. Leigh's corner of the room came what was unmistakably a laugh. "What's so funny?" Miss Firenze said.

"I'm sorry. I intended to cough."

"Then why didn't you? You laughed."

"Is that how it sounded? I've always had a very peculiar cough, probably environmental."

"She has an explanation for everything," Miss Firenze told Michael. "And she uses big words to impress me. Well, I ain't impressed. One of these days I'm going to kick her out on her ass. . . . Do you have good teeth, Mr. Minister?"

"Good enough."

"How often do you clean them?"

"Whenever I have the chance."

"Smile."

He smiled uneasily, aware that somehow in the past few minutes he had lost control of the situation and the old lady, crazy or not, had taken charge.

"Does Madam wish me to tape this?" Ms. Leigh said.

"This what?"

"For lack of a better word, conversation."

"You see?" The old lady appealed to Michael again. "She's being sarcastic as usual. Beats me how I stand her around. I could never figure out these Orientals. Their face does one thing while their brain does another. What's more, they're all flat-chested."

Ms. Leigh let out another of her peculiar coughs, excused herself and left the room.

"Now," the old lady said. "Now you and I can talk. What's on your mind?"

"I—"

"You didn't come here to save my soul, did you? Waste of time, boy, waste of time. I don't have one. A chaplain told me that once. He didn't have much of a soul himself, just a hankering like any swabbie. He was a navy chaplain. Were you ever in the navy?"

"No."

"Do you hanker?"

"Yes."

"Got a wife?"

95

"Yes."

"You're not much of a talker, are you?"

"I haven't had much of a chance."

"Okay, it's your turn. Say something."

There was a brief silence before Michael spoke again. "I suppose I could claim that this is strictly a social call but it isn't. I came here in the hope of getting some information."

"What about?"

"You do some exploring around the neighborhood, I'm told."

"Sure I do, whenever they're not looking. I don't know why I'm penned up like this anyway. I think it's that guy at the bank. He's got some fancy title but what it boils down to is money. *My* money. He's afraid I might throw it away or something. And you know what he does with it? *He* throws it away on a pack of lawyers and this bunch of nuts who're supposed to be looking after me. Does that make sense?"

"When you put it like that, no."

"Then you're on my side."

"I believe I am," Michael said, sounding a little surprised.

The old lady raised herself from the pillows and sat up, clasping her knees with her hands. Her fingernails, painted the same red as her lipstick, were so long they curled inward like claws.

"You and I will work together, boy. Between the two of us we'll beat the bank, the cops, the lawyers, we'll take on the whole damn navy. How about it?"

"I don't think I'm equipped for that big a job."

"Okay, let's start nice and easy at the beginning. First we get the hell out of here."

"Well, I—"

"What's the matter, losing your nerve before we even start?"

"Having me along would cramp your style," Michael said. "Besides, a less direct approach might be more successful."

"Stop the wishy-washy talk. What do you mean?"

"I'm referring to the book Miss Firenze is writing."

"Oh that, sure. Sure, that'll teach the navy a thing or two, but it's taking so long. I want action now. Today."

"What day is it, Miss Firenze?"

"Oh, maybe Tuesday, Wednesday, somewhere along in there."

It was Thursday. "What month is it?"

"It's cold, maybe winter. Why are you asking me? Go look at a calendar."

Her nails picked at her black robe as if they were scratching the earth for insects.

"Miss Firenze."

"Why are you asking me a bunch of dumb questions?"

"I'm trying to find out what happened to the little girl who lived in the house across the canyon."

"How should I know? I never took on little girls, never a one less than fourteen years old and then only if some of my bitches tried to go in business for themselves leaving me short-handed."

"Annamay Hyatt was eight years old." But even as he spoke he realized how useless it was to ask any further questions. She didn't know what day it was, or what month, probably not even what year. How could she remember seeing Annamay at any particular time? Perhaps she had never seen her at all.

"I hate kids, always have," Miss Firenze said confidentially. "Ms. Leigh warned me never to say that in front of anyone, especially those cops who were crawling all over the place. But it's true. She said I'd better shut my mouth or they'd put me in prison. They can't put me in prison for hating kids, can they?"

"No."

"Besides, where the hell do you think I am now, with bars on the windows and gates kept locked? I'm thinking of running away and getting married."

"How will you manage that?"

"Never you mind. I'm a practical woman. Cheap, some call me. Let them." She reached for a folded paper napkin on the night table beside the bed. "Guess what's in here."

"I can't."

"Try."

"A piece of jewelry, perhaps?"

"You think I'm stupid or something, keeping jewelry lying around in a house with a pack of thieves in it? This"— she waved the napkin at him—"is something left over from breakfast. That's your clue."

"I'm afraid it doesn't help much."

"Give up?"

"Yes."

She opened the napkin which contained what appeared to be several dark stones. For a moment he thought they might be part of her collection of gallstones she kept in the cigar box along with her teeth and wedding ring.

"Raisins," she said triumphantly. "Ha, fooled you, didn't I? Raisins. I saved them from my bran cereal this morning. You never can tell when the champagne's going to go flat. I watched many a buck disappear in thin air until I discovered the secret of raisins."

"I wasn't aware raisins had a secret."

"Oh yes. I found out from one of my girls. When a magnum of champagne goes flat you drop in a couple of raisins and like magic up come the bubbles again."

"Is that a fact?"

"Usually. Sometimes you hit a rotten raisin. But these look pretty good, don't you think?"

"Yes. Now about the little girl who disappeared—"

"Many little girls disappear," Miss Firenze said sternly. "Many more should. Also dogs, horses, cats, cows. The world's getting too damn full. There isn't enough champagne for everyone." She rewrapped the raisins in the napkin and hid them in a drawer of the night table. Because, she explained, you never knew when that flat-chested Oriental might discover the magic power of raisins and no cereal would ever be safe from her again. "If I got married again," Miss Firenze said, "I wouldn't have to put up with all this disrespect. My husband would be in charge of my affairs and that silly ass at the bank could go poop in his soup. The last time I asked him for a few thousand dollars to go to Europe to trace my roots he turned me down flat. My name sounds Italian but I think I'm Turkish or Roumanian or something along in there. I'll never find out for sure until I get married."

"How will that help you?"

"I told you before, my husband will take charge of my affairs. And I don't have to ask the bank or the lawyer for permission to get married either. I'm over twenty-one, in case you haven't noticed." She giggled into her cupped hands like an embarrassed teenager. "Don't you think marriage is a good idea?"

"That would depend on the man involved."

"Oh, he's very proper. A gentleman, and at least as old as I am. Don't imagine for a minute I have my eye on any of these young pipsqueaks around here out looking for a fortune. I told you, I'm a practical woman."

Michael was accustomed to dealing with people who were disturbed to some degree and Miss Firenze didn't faze him. But trying to pick his way through her facts and fantasies made him a little dizzy. He said, "Does the gentleman know of your intentions?"

"There is an unspoken agreement."

"Why is the agreement unspoken?"

"Because we've never had a chance to talk. I can't get out through this pack of nitwits and he can't get in. But he's ripe and ready."

"What makes you think so?"

"He spies on me all the time through a telescope. Sends me passionate glances from his spy tower."

Michael realized with a shock that she was referring to Howard's father. "How do you know this, Miss Firenze?"

"Because I can *see* him. I've got these binoculars a vice admiral gave me years ago. They're very powerful, ten by fifty he told me, and so heavy I can hardly lift them. I keep them on the windowsill. The gentleman waves to me over the treetops and I wave back to him over the treetops. It's very romantic."

"What is his name?"

"I don't know. He doesn't know mine either. Oh, we'll exchange names before we're married, of course, because he'll have to sign a heap of blah-blah papers for the lawyers. He seems like a nice old chap. Likes fish. Sits beside the pond and stares at fish. Well, I can overlook that. I'm a little peculiar myself at times."

"Mr. Hyatt is the little girl's grandfather."

"What little girl?"

"The one I referred to before."

"I don't know any such girl. You keep accusing me of using little girls in my business and I never did. I never used one that was less than fourteen, never. Don't you bad-mouth me, minister man, hypocrite, liar. You get out of here. Get out or I'll scream. I'll scream rape, you son of a bitch." And she threw back her head and opened her mouth and screamed.

The sound chased him out the door and down the stairs like a siren in pursuit.

Ms. Leigh was waiting for him in the tiled hall, along with a muscular young white-coated attendant. Neither of them looked in the least perturbed.

"Jeez, he really *is* a minister," the attendant said, raising his voice so he could be heard above the old lady's continued screams. "Okay, I owe you five."

"If you didn't bet on everything, George, you wouldn't lose so often."

"I thought you were bluffing again, or kidding."

"I'll take the five now."

"I haven't got—"

"You got."

"Nobody trusts me anymore."

"Nobody ever did, George."

"It's not fair. I thought you were trying to bluff me the way you always do. You came back to the kitchen and said Madam had a caller and you thought he was a minister. And I said, five bucks he's not. I thought I had a sure thing."

"You do have a sure thing, George. It's called terminal gullibility. Pay up."

George paid up and departed in the direction of Miss Firenze's room. His lack of haste indicated that the situation was not uncommon.

"Soooo," Ms. Leigh said, pursing her lips, "your rapport with Firenze didn't last very long. That's the trouble with flaky ladies. They never flake and unflake on schedule. What happened?"

"I asked her a question she didn't like."

"About her past?"

"Evidently she thought so but it wasn't. It concerned Annamay Hyatt."

"Oh." Ms. Leigh took off her glasses and rubbed them on the sleeve of her green sweater as though to clean up some invisible spots that were blurring her vision. "No, she wouldn't like that. The case affected her very badly right from the beginning. Whenever anything about it was shown on television she'd throw a fit. And if she overheard any of us talking about it around the house she'd fire us. I must have been fired twenty times at least but since she hasn't the power to hire or fire I'm still here."

"Why did she react so violently?"

"It's her nature to react violently to anything which displeases her. She had no relationship with the little girl, at least to my knowledge. I doubt she'd ever even seen her. The attendants are careful to keep children away because

Firenze doesn't like them. They make her nervous. She often refers to them in her fits of fear. Children are part of the 'they' who are out to get her. There are many such references in my notes, especially on days when she's escaped and something has frightened her like a sudden storm or the fog rolling in."

"Could you look up some of these references for me?"

"I could. It would take time." Ms. Leigh replaced her glasses. "My husband Larry's drama lessons are very expensive."

"You'll be paid for your time, of course."

"Like how much?"

"Maybe not enough to turn Larry into another Dustin Hoffman but a reasonable amount."

"Larry's taller than Hoffman and better looking."

"Then it won't require quite so much money, will it?" Michael said. "How about twenty-five an hour, plus a bonus for quick work?"

"Sounds fair. I'll give it my best shot. But don't expect miracles. Most of the stuff, or a lot of it anyway, is the ranting of a nutty old lady who's afraid of her past catching up with her."

"But mixed up with the ranting may be some kernels of truth. To the child's father," Michael added, "one kernel is better than nothing. It's possible that Miss Firenze witnessed something on the day Annamay disappeared. She was never questioned by the police, you know, because her lawyers wouldn't permit it."

"Naturally not. She would have told one cock-and-bull story after another in order to remain the center of attention. They could have believed one of them. And indeed, some might even have been true. But it's not likely. She doesn't usually tell the truth when she's basking in the limelight, only when she's scared. That's when she lets out things she normally hides, like her real age, which is seventy-eight not seventy-three, and the name of her first and last husband,

Joe Willie Smith, a black army private who was killed in Korea. Official documents don't list either of those facts."

"How can you be sure they're facts?"

Ms. Leigh said, with a faint smile. "All us flat-chested Orientals have ESP, didn't you know that?"

"I'm learning."

"Around here you need ESP. Firenze is a very convincing liar because she actually believes herself."

"Does she ever go across the creek and into the Hyatts' avocado grove?"

"I guess she's covered the whole area at one time or another. We get a complaint now and then from someone in the neighborhood, but mostly she just walks along the creek and picks flowers and grass and things."

Miss Firenze's screaming had stopped abruptly and George appeared at the head of the stairs.

"Hey, Leigh, tote your tush up here. She wants to see you."

"Tell her I'll be right there." Ms. Leigh offered her hand to Michael. "Do you mind letting yourself out? She's often calm after one of these storms and I get some usable material. How do I get in touch with you?"

Michael gave her both his own number and that of the Hyatts' guest cottage. "Call any time."

"Very well, I'll see what I can do, Mr. Dunlop."

"Thank you."

They shook hands again and Michael went out the door. The Oasis Pool Service truck was still parked outside the house, joined now by All-American Tree Service and Channel Hospital and Uniform Supplies. The same two gardeners were clipping the same privet hedge. The hedge appeared to go on and on, with no end in sight in either direction, and the gardeners were apparently content to go on and on with it. Perhaps they would continue right into spring when the privet bloomed and they were forced away by swarms of bees and the oversweet odor of the flowers.

Halfway down the driveway he turned and looked back at the villa. Madam Firenze had stepped out on her balcony on the second floor and was waving at him in a friendly but formal way like royalty acknowledging her subjects.

He didn't wave back.

When he returned through the Hyatts' avocado grove the dogs came running to greet him, the shepherd barking hysterically, the Newfoundland silent and placid as usual. They both looked neglected. Newf's feathered legs and plumed tail had collected dozens of burr clovers and Shep's underbelly was shafted with foxtails. Burr clover was a relatively harmless nuisance to animals but foxtails could do serious damage, digging farther and farther into the skin as if they were alive. Michael picked them all out carefully, keeping them in his hand until he could find a trash can to prevent them from reseeding.

The palace too looked neglected, its windows smudged, its patch of lawn dried out, the barbecue pit choked with eucalyptus pods and pine needles and sycamore leaves. There were no fish in the fishpond and only an inch or two of dirty water.

The front door was partly open as though someone had forgotten to lock it and it had been pushed inward by the wind or one of the dogs or a reconnoitering possum. When Michael went to close it he saw that sycamore leaves were scattered around the room, on the small davenport and dining set and stove, even on the bunk beds where Marietta and Luella Lu lay awaiting their mistress. Marietta's half-bald head was partly covered by a leaf that looked quite like a perky new hat. Luella Lu had been turned on her side and her glued eye was staring straight at Michael and beyond.

The two dogs, Shep strangely silent, sat outside the door, as though they had forgotten they were ever allowed inside as the royal attendants. Michael, who'd never owned a dog, had felt no real kinship with one until this moment when he wondered how much of Annamay was still alive inside their heads, a voice, a touch, a smell, a laugh.

He closed the door and began walking along the path toward the main house with the dogs following. If they hadn't suddenly bounded off in the direction of the koi pond he would have missed the old man sitting beside it.

"Good morning, Michael," Mr. Hyatt said.

"Good morning, Mr. Hyatt."

"Then it was you thrashing around in the avocado grove."

"I didn't realize I was thrashing."

"But you were. I have very good hearing. It's lucky you chose the profession you did. You would have made a very poor Indian scout."

"I quite agree."

"Of course some leaves are very numerous and noisy this late in the year, at least until the first rain. Then they go soft and cling to the earth until they are a part of it again." Mr. Hyatt's face was almost hidden by a crudely woven straw hat, the kind the Mexican pickers used. "It was that unseasonal rain in late July that prevented her from being found sooner. The leaves became soft and pliant and clung to her. And the earth claimed her for its own without us even knowing about it. You said it well at the funeral. Would you repeat it for me, please?"

"Of dust we are made and to dust we shall return."

"Yes. Yes, even the koi here can't live forever. But how they do try. In Japan where they are passed along from generation to generation like heirlooms, koi are much admired for their longevity and courage. One requires the other, you know. It isn't easy to grow old. I believe the record among koi is two hundred and twenty-eight years. The magoi here, the black fellow, is already older than I am."

"I can't see him."

"He's lying at the bottom, perhaps sleeping, certainly not thinking. They're very stupid, actually. Some people think that because they will come to the side of the pool when you clap your hands and offer them food that they are trained. Not so. They're only eating. Watch." Mr. Hyatt clapped his hands, then brought from his pocket some bits of what looked like dog kibble. He tossed them into the water. The brighter-colored koi came immediately to eat. Then the magoi appeared and the others moved aside to make way for him.

"Some people might think," Mr. Hyatt said, "that they are showing respect for their elders in the Oriental tradition. Nonsense. He is simply bigger than they are. Notice the slow grace with which he moves, as if he had all the time in the world. And certainly he has a great deal, perhaps another hundred years. And what for? It doesn't make sense. He serves no useful purpose in the scheme of things, his brain is minimal. Nature has made some dreadful errors, allowing valuable human beings to die so young, and this creature to go on and on."

The black magoi ate a couple of pellets of food. He was as large as a turkey and had a fat sad face with two drooping whiskers on each side of his O-shaped mouth. In the center of his forehead was a spot the exact size and color of a five-dollar gold piece. The old man looked at the magoi bitterly as though he were begrudging it the years that had been taken from Annamay.

Michael said, "The fishpond at the palace is empty."

"Yes. I emptied it myself. Raccoons ate all the goldfish. They'd get the koi too but the water is too deep. A raccoon must have water shallow enough for him to stand upright in order to catch fish."

"Mr. Hyatt—"

"Useless," the old man said. "Not even beautiful unless you count the gold piece on his head. All creatures become useless as they grow old. Someone should have an answer."

"Perhaps there isn't one."

"You should work on it, Michael."

"I'll try," Michael said. He hesitated to bring up the subject of the palace door's being open, but decided it was necessary. "I found the door of the palace open, Mr. Hyatt."

"You don't mean actually open, do you? You must be referring to the fact that the Sheriff's Department removed the seal some time ago."

"The door was open."

"That's impossible. I locked it myself the day I emptied the fishpond." The old man sounded calm enough but his hands had begun to tremble. "Did you look inside?"

"Briefly."

"Was there evidence of an intruder?"

"Some leaves and dirt had been blown in by the wind. Whether anything is missing I don't know."

"Someone broke in," the old man whispered. "Someone broke into my Annamay's palace."

"It's more likely that you forgot to lock it, Mr. Hyatt."

"No, no. I did not. People are always accusing me of forgetting this and forgetting that and sometimes they are correct. I do forget things now and then. But never, never would I forget to lock the palace." He shook his head so vigorously that the straw hat slid down his face and fell on the grass. He didn't seem to notice. "It is my most important duty. My son, Howard, thinks up all kinds of duties for me because he thinks they will make me happier. And I do them because that makes *him* happier. It is a game we play, pretending I am still of some value in this world."

"That's not the way—"

"Please, Michael, don't argue the point. It would be a waste of time. I have done more thinking about this business of age than you have, perhaps more than you'll ever have a chance to. My son and daughter-in-law love me, true. But if I died tomorrow I would leave no noticeable gap because I have no real place in the world, no real duties to perform. My only real duty is to keep the palace as Annamay left it. I allow no one in, not even Dru. Dru used to come sometimes and peer into the windows as if she thought Annamay might be in there hiding from us all. She knows better now. She was at the funeral."

"The lock on the door is a simple one," Michael said. "Nearly anybody could pick it."

"Do people no longer respect a locked door?"

"I'm afraid not, Mr. Hyatt."

"The world has become a rough place. Perhaps it is better that Annamay never found that out. To her every day was sunny, every stranger was her friend." He put the battered straw hat back on, pulling it well down on his forehead so Michael couldn't see the moisture in his eyes. "We'd better go and have a look at the palace. It must be kept as Annamay left it."

Mr. Hyatt rose unsteadily from the redwood chair, refusing Michael's offer of an arm to help him.

"Don't," he said sharply. "Don't start treating me the way Howard does. I'm not decrepit. Indeed, only the other day I helped an elderly woman across the creek. I felt like a boy scout again, especially when she offered me a bouquet of flowers."

"Did you know the woman?"

"I've seen her." He nodded in the direction of the villa. "She lives over there and they say she is quite mad. But they say things about everyone. Who is to judge?"

"In this case a judge," Michael said. "She has been declared incompetent by the court."

"Incompetent to do what?"

"Handle her own affairs. Financial affairs, I presume."

"Bless you, Michael. I know hundreds and hundreds of people who are incompetent to handle their own financial affairs. Pillars of society, politicians, educators, they bet on commodities like racehorses and can't tell a stock from a bond. But are they declared incompetent? No indeed. . . . They are reappointed, reaffirmed, reelected."

"Miss Firenze's incompetence goes beyond financial matters, I assure you."

"You've seen her, talked to her?"

"Yes."

The two men had begun walking toward the palace but now Mr. Hyatt stopped and grabbed Michael by the arm. "Did you ask her about Annamay?"

"Yes."

"Did she know anything?"

"No."

"No one knows anything. A little girl disappears and her body is not found for months. *This* is incompetence. Why doesn't the court do something about *this* kind of incompetence?" He lowered his voice. "You and Howard are working on the case, aren't you?"

"Yes."

"I heard you talking last night when I passed the guest cottage and the windows were open."

The previous night had been cold and Michael distinctly recalled Howard's closing the windows on both sides. But if Mr. Hyatt chose to remember it another way there was no use correcting him.

"Why don't you and Howard take me into your confidence, Michael?"

"There is nothing to confide so far."

"But you will take me into your confidence when the time comes?"

"That will depend on Howard. It's his decision."

"Then I'll be kept in the dark," the old man said sadly. "If I ask questions Howard will merely send me away on one of my so-called duties, charting a bunch of silly boats passing in the channel, or driving to the post office or anything else to get me out of the way because I am a nuisance. I am as useless as the magoi, taking up space, killing time until it kills me."

"Howard loves and respects and admires you, Mr. Hyatt."

"He used to. At one time I deserved respect and a certain amount of admiration, perhaps even some love."

"I hate to hear you talking like this, Mr. Hyatt."

"Of course you do, Michael. Ministers are the last people in the world who want to hear the truth. It so often disputes their version of the world."

When they reached the palace Mr. Hyatt opened the front door. Leaves stirred and rustled like living creatures scurrying away to hide from danger.

"Someone has been here, Michael. There are signs. One of the dolls is lying on her side and I left her on her back. And the cushions on the davenport are out of place. And look here, a teacup in the sink. All the dishes were stored in the cupboard when I left. There are other signs, little things I can't quite put my finger on. But I know. I *know*."

He was breathing so hard and fast by this time that Michael, afraid he was going to have a heart attack, tried to persuade him to sit down. But he refused to sit. He began opening and closing drawers and cupboards and closets. In the main closet with the sliding door several of Annamay's dresses were still hanging, as well as larger-sized clothes (Kay's? Chizzy's?) used to play grown-up. There were a couple of mismatched sneakers, some socks and a sweater, and, tossed into a corner, a pair of high-heeled sandals. They were both large and wide, with rhinestone straps and heels narrow as nails.

"Those peculiar shoes," Mr. Hyatt said. "I've never seen them before."

"They're probably Kay's or Chizzy's."

"Dear me, no. Kay would never wear such trollopy things, and Chizzy couldn't walk across a room in heels like that without breaking her neck. Besides, they're much too big for her."

"Annamay might have borrowed them from one of the maids."

"The maids are all Mexican, short in stature, with small hands and feet. These look as if they might belong to a tall black woman but there are no tall black women on the staff."

Michael took the shoes out of the closet and examined them. They were almost brand-new, bearing only a few scratches on the soles. He put them back in the closet and closed the door.

"I never saw those shoes before," Mr. Hyatt repeated. "But perhaps I merely overlooked them and they've been here all along."

"Perhaps."

"Do you think we should clean the place up a bit before we go?"

"No. A few leaves and a little dirt won't hurt anything and I think Howard should see the room as it is."

"Why?"

"He might want to ask the police to go over it for signs of forced entry."

The old man was silent a moment. "No, Michael. Howard has lost his faith in the police. And who can blame him? They've made no arrests and even the people detained for questioning have been let go within a few hours. Yet they must know, as Howard knows, and I know in my heart, that one of those people is guilty. . . . Do you believe a person is innocent until proven guilty?"

"The law says so and I must abide by it."

"That wasn't my question. I didn't use the word *abide*. You abide, certainly. But do you believe a person is innocent until proven guilty?"

"No."

"You're aware of dozens of guilty people walking around the streets, even sitting in your congregation. Aren't you?"

"Yes."

Mr. Hyatt locked the door of the palace and returned the keyring to his pocket. Then he began walking back toward the main house, shaking his head with each step like a mechanical man, a toy soldier without a war.

Michael left him where he'd found him, in the redwood chair beside the koi pond. The multicolored koi were still swimming aimlessly round and round but the old black giant had gone back to his hideout in the deepest darkest water.

Chapter SEVEN

Chizzy was cooking again.

While cleaning out the freezer she'd come across five pounds of hamburger which had to be used because it had passed the expiration date on the label. She cooked the whole batch in a Dutch oven, added onions and tomatoes and various spices, and divided the meat into four casseroles. To one she added rice and to another pinto beans. Noodles went into the third and bulgur into the last.

Then, faced with the four casseroles, she sat down and had a good cry because there was no one to eat them. Kay had gone to dinner with Ben York, Mr. Hyatt said he wasn't hungry, and Howard had shut himself up in the guest cottage, leaving a note on the kitchen table that he was not to be disturbed. She knew Michael was there too because she'd heard his car on the driveway. His car was as noisy as Ben's but not in the same way. Ben's gave the impression of speed and power; Michael's coughed and gasped and wheezed like an old gasoholic having one final binge.

Chizzy cried as quickly and efficiently as she did her housework, and pretty soon it was over and she rubbed her face briskly with a wet towel. Then she decided on a sensible apportionment of the casseroles. One she would deliver to Howard and Michael personally since she did not include herself in any Do Not Disturb notes. She would store one in the refrigerator and take another over to Ernestina, the maid next door, who would probably add chili powder and jalapeños and ruin the whole thing. Mrs. Cunningham down the street was considered briefly as a recipient of the fourth, but her reaction to the meat loaf had been so peculiar that Chizzy decided to eat the casserole herself. She left it in the oven to keep warm while she carried Howard's over to the guest cottage, wearing the padded mitts she used for barbecues.

It was seven o'clock. Fog had rolled in from the sea before sunset and the gray night was somehow more sinister than any plain black one. Though she never would have admitted it, Chizzy was afraid of the night anyway. She turned on all the little lights that lined the garden paths and took the two dogs with her for protection.

The vertical venetian blinds of the guest cottage were angled shut but light squeezed out from the sides. Though the windows were closed she could hear voices inside, Howard's and Michael's and a third voice, louder than the others and higher-pitched. Holding the casserole close to her chest for warmth and comfort, she knocked on the door with the toe of her shoe.

There was immediate silence, then Howard's voice:

"Who is it?"

"Me. I brought you a—"

"Didn't you get the note not to disturb me?"

"Yes. But I didn't think you meant me."

"It was addressed to you."

"I thought you might mean, oh, sort of the public in general."

"The public in general doesn't have access to my kitchen."

Someone in the room laughed, certainly not Howard and probably not Michael. That left the stranger. She didn't know what he could be laughing at. Nothing funny had been said and there was certainly nothing funny about standing out in a cold gray night being rebuked like an ordinary servant. She felt her face redden.

"You open this door immediately, Mr. Howard," she said in the firm tone she used on the dogs. "I brought you and the Reverend some supper and I don't intend to stay out here all night holding it."

The door opened about a foot. "All right, Chizzy. Thank you."

"Put it in the oven at three hundred degrees until you're ready to eat."

"I'm ready now," the stranger said and laughed again.

He was sitting in a lounge chair beside a floor lamp. The lamp was turned on full and she had a good view of him but she could hardly make out his features. His eyes were almost concealed by a pair of dark bushy brows that met on the bridge of his nose, and his mouth was merely a line of separation between his straggly moustache and his long full beard. His hair reached his shoulders and only the fact that it was iron-gray gave any indication that he was middle-aged or more. She was sure of one thing, however. He had been drinking. The place smelled like a winery.

Chizzy crossed the room to the kitchenette alcove and put the casserole in the oven, uneasily aware that the stranger was watching her.

"That's her," he said. "The little fat lady that chased me with a broom, screaming like a banshee."

"I did no such thing," Chizzy protested. "I never saw you before in my life."

"I was wearing my professional costume for the benefit of the summer tourists. A white robe makes me look more like a prophet."

"How could I sound like one of those things when I've never seen one even in a zoo?"

"The banshee is a spirit, madam. It wails and screams outside a house to warn the occupants of an approaching death."

Chizzy stood in the middle of the room, her hands raised. She was still wearing the oven mitts, but now they looked like specially designed boxing gloves.

"That's wrongful talk in front of people still in mourning, mister."

"I was only passing along some information, nothing personal intended."

"You keep your nasty information to yourself. No one here wants it."

She had more to say on the subject and was preparing to say it when Howard took her by the arm and guided her to the door. Almost before she realized it she was back in the cold gray night, angry and humiliated. She had been insulted by a stranger, rebuked by Howard, and the minister hadn't even opened his mouth to defend her, let alone thank her for the food.

In addition to all this, the dogs had abandoned her, gone off on some business of their own. Starting back along the path to the house she heard Shep give a couple of loud sharp barks and then, uncharacteristically, lapse into silence.

The silence worried her. Once Shep started barking he kept it up until it was out of his system, having run its course like a head cold. She had a dreadful image of someone grabbing him and holding his mouth closed or choking the breath out of him. She almost fainted with relief when he suddenly reappeared on the path in front of her, good as new, wagging his tail.

Mr. Hyatt stepped out from behind an escallonia shrub looking like a piece of the night in his old gray tweed suit.

"Chizzy?"

"You gave me a fright," she said crossly. "You're supposed to be in the house watching the seven o'clock news."

"I watched the six o'clock news," he said. "And the five o'clock news."

"Well, you shouldn't be out here slurking around in the bushes."

"Slurking?"

She knew from his tone that there was something wrong with the word but she couldn't tell what, so she repeated it decisively to make it sound more authentic. "Slurking's what they called it in my family. Anyway, Mr. Howard wouldn't like such behavior."

"I saw the garden-path lights go on and I wanted to find out what was happening."

"Nothing is happening."

"You went into the cottage."

"I took some food."

"What are they up to in there?"

"I don't know." She put her hand on his arm, intending to guide him back to the house. Instead, she found herself clinging to him. "Mr. Hyatt. I don't *know*. They have an awful-looking man with them. He called me names like fat and said I chased him with a broom and screamed like a banshee."

"You are a bit on the stocky side," the old man said gently. "And you have quite a formidable voice. Did you ever take lessons?"

"No, but I sang in the Pentecostal choir for six years."

"That explains it then."

"It was a very good choir, if you'll excuse the bragging. One Christmas we made a record and sent it to the President. He sent us a thank-you letter in return. I forget who was President back then but it was a very nice letter. The choirmaster had it framed and hung on the wall."

She was suddenly feeling much better, not a fat vindictive screamer, but a member of a choir singled out by the President of the United States for special commendation.

"Now you better skedaddle on into the house," she said, brushing off the sleeve of his jacket as if to remove any traces of her clutching him. "You can catch the rest of the seven o'clock news."

"I watched the five o'clock news," he said again, "and the

six o'clock news." And very likely he would watch the ten o'clock, and if he was still awake, the eleven o'clock. It would all be the same news, in different voices.

The visitor settled back in the lounge chair, feeling comfortable and relaxed. The room was pleasant, his host polite and soft-voiced, and the food the old biddy had brought over smelled enticing. Since no one had offered him any he decided a hint or two was in order.

"I haven't had a square meal in a while," he told Howard. "November's a bad month for tourists, and they're my main source of income."

"You can eat later," Howard said. He glanced at the sheet of paper Michael handed him. "Cassius Cassandra. Is that your real name?"

"It's the name I'm known by. You come down to my end of town and ask for Cassius or Mr. Cassandra, everybody knows who you mean. Ask for Desmond Walsh and they never heard of him. That's the name on my birth certificate, Desmond Thomas Walsh."

"Do you know why you're here, Mr. Walsh?"

"Sure do. I was paid. Some in advance from him"—he indicated Michael sitting at the table—"and the rest to come from you."

"What are you being paid to do?"

"Tell the truth. Which is a funny thing when you come to think about it. The Cassandra in Greek legend always told the truth, only nobody ever believed it."

"Cassandra predicted the future," Howard said. "All I want from you is the past."

"What if I don't say what you want to hear? Do I get paid anyway?"

"Yes."

"Fair enough. Let's get started."

"Mr. Dunlop and I have obtained a copy of the statement

you gave to the police in August. I'd like to see how it compares with what you remember now."

The prospect of being caught in a lie didn't seem to bother Walsh. "There'll be differences here and there. Truth is relative. And when the cops questioned me I was scared as hell of a possible child-molesting charge. That can be rough. Even in the holding tank before you get a chance to enter a plea, if the word goes out that you may be a child molester, you're in for a bad time from the other prisoners. Short eyes, that's what molesters are called. Among other things."

"Has such a charge ever been brought against you, Mr. Walsh?"

"No, sir. I don't deny I've seen the inside of a few holding tanks over the years, what with one thing and another. Booze mainly, nothing heavy."

"Do you know who I am and where you are?"

"Mr. Dunlop told me on the way over from my hotel."

"Have you been on this property before?"

"Once. That was when the little fat lady chased me with a broom."

"What brought you here?"

"I was going to help myself to a couple of avocados. Not pick any, you understand, just gather up some windfalls. Also I like to get out in the country once in a while and this is as close to country as you can get without a car or bike. So I came here."

"And after gathering up a few windfalls you left the property?"

"I intended to. Then through the trees I saw that cute little house and I thought maybe a midget lived there. I used to know a midget when I was traveling with a carnival. He called himself Paul Bunyan, Junior. Cranky little bastard, always bitching that the world was too big for him. I used to cool him down with doses of philosophy. Listen man, I'd tell

119

him, the world is too big for any of us. He liked that kind of talk. He was a deep thinker."

"Did you enter the small house?"

"No. The fat lady showed up with two ferocious-looking dogs. I wasn't scared of the dogs because they were both wagging their tails. But the old girl meant business. Women have a violent streak in them."

"Are you married, Mr. Walsh?"

Walsh thought about it. "What did I tell the police?"

"Let's hear what you have to say now."

"Not much of anything, actually. I'm not sure if I'm married or not. My last wife took off for Mexico with some guy she met at a bingo game. Maybe she got a divorce, maybe not."

"After you were chased off this property, did you return?"

"I think I told the police I never came to the premises again. But that doesn't mean I didn't come *near* the premises again."

"Did you?"

"Sure. I must have walked along the creek half a dozen times, cooling my feet and thinking. All kinds of people go there. Flowing water has a fascination for nearly everyone. Maybe it's because, as Heraclitus wrote, all things are in a state of flux."

"Are you still in the habit of walking along the creek?"

"No. Sitting here in this room, this is the closest I've come in a long time."

"Why?"

"The little girl disappeared. After that everything changed. It wasn't good clean country anymore. The water looked dirty and I felt like there was a cop behind every tree."

"Did you ever talk to my daughter, Annamay?"

"I talked to a little blond girl. I didn't know her name until I saw her picture in the paper after she disappeared.

She was a nice friendly little girl, full of questions. All kids are curious about my tambourine. I told her I bang on it to attract attention. It's part of my professional equipment. You can't make prophecies without an audience and that's my way of gathering an audience. Prophesying is my business, though the cops may call it panhandling or even extortion. It's certainly not extortion. If I'm standing in front of a shop making prophecies and the shop owner pays me to move along, that's not extortion. It's common sense on his part and a way of staying off the welfare rolls on mine. Or maybe I follow a couple of tourists down the street announcing the world will self-destruct tomorrow or something else they don't want to hear because they still have a week's vacation left. They may slip me a little change to go away. Now I don't claim this is a high-class way of making a living but it's just as honest as some, not excluding yours, Mr. Hyatt. Financial predictions often have no more basis than my prophecies. As for you, sir"—he pointed a finger at Michael. The tip of it was missing, as though it had been chopped off by some unhappy recipient of his prophecies—"you and your kind carry on about heaven and hell and then take up a collection. You know why people put money on a collection plate? Fear. The same reason why the shop owner and the tourist pay me. But nobody calls your racket extortion."

"You might be surprised," Michael said wryly.

"Some do, eh?"

"Some do."

"So we are all three of us, relatively speaking, in the same boat. Mr. Hyatt occupies the best seat. But if the boat springs a leak he's going to get just as wet as the rest of us."

"Is that one of your prophecies, Mr. Walsh?"

"No, sir. It's the simple truth."

"As you pointed out a few minutes ago, truth is relative."

"There are a few basic facts we must all confront."

"All right, let's see you confront one," Howard said. "In the early afternoon on the day my daughter disappeared, you were observed by one of the homeowners in the area as you walked along the north side of the creek. Mr. Cunningham was on the edge of his property looking for his cat."

"Maybe he was looking for his cat, maybe he was looking for one of his chickens who'd flown the coop. And I don't mean the kind with feathers. Anyway, he was shouting the name Randy. Not loud, kind of coaxing-like. As soon as he spotted me he went back up the hill toward his house."

"And what did you do, Mr. Walsh?"

"I sat on the bank and watched the water flowing past me. It's better than watching the waves break on shore because there you get the impression it's always the same water, over and over, day after day. But water flowing down a river or a creek is always different. Every drop that passes you is different. I bet Heraclitus sat on a lot of riverbanks."

"How long were you there?"

"I can't recall exactly but it wasn't long because suddenly it got very still and quiet. Then it started up, the desert wind like a blast from some hell on the other side of the mountain. You never can tell about those devil winds. Sometimes they stop pretty quick, sometimes they keep blowing for hours. I waited around for a while, then I could feel my throat drying up and my sinuses clogging, so I wet my handkerchief and wrapped it around my face and got out of there. I went back to my hotel room and closed the windows and blinds and watched the soaps. You can't fight a devil wind. It'll blow the skin right off you if you give it a chance."

"Were you wearing your so-called professional costume at the time?"

"Yes. That's how the cops found me so easy after Cunningham told them about seeing me. Not many men in town wear a white robe and carry a tambourine. In the long run though, it proved to my advantage. If I was planning any mischief would I have worn something that could identify me like that? The newspapers made out that it was real detective work on the part of the cops to find me so fast. I don't mind giving credit where credit is due, but the fact is, a one-eyed drunken imbecile could have found me. And maybe one did." Walsh's moustache moved up and down at the corners in what appeared to be a smile.

"You don't get along with the police, Mr. Walsh?"

"Sure I do. I get along with everybody. It's just that I resent them treating me like a lunatic when I'm actually a legitimate businessman like yourself. My way of making a living may be somewhat eccentric but then look at you, playing around with paper money. And him"— Walsh pointed his mutilated finger at Michael again— "Look at you rattling the cages of people's souls. If one among us must be considered a lunatic, then I would be the obvious choice. But would I be the real one? Think about it."

There was a silence while everybody presumably thought about it. But Walsh didn't like silences, especially his own. He said, "That stuff the little fat lady brought over is beginning to smell better and better. Would it be presumptuous of me to ask for a small helping?"

"I'm going to call a taxi to take you home," Howard said. "You'll have time to eat while you're waiting for it."

"I can't be seen arriving back at my hotel in a taxi. Most people there think I own my own car. I let them think so. It gives me a little more clout."

"You can tell the driver to let you off a block away."

"All right."

Howard opened a bottle of wine and Michael took the casserole out of the oven, using a couple of towels as pot-holders. Then the table was cleared of papers and the three men sat down to eat.

Walsh proposed the toast.

"Here's to you and here's to me,
And may we never disagree.
But if by any chance we do,
Here's to me, and the hell with you."

It was more truth than prophecy.

By nine o'clock he was gone and another name was crossed
off the list—Cassius Cassandra, Seabreeze Hotel, occupation, prophet. Several names had already been crossed off,
including the one immediately above it: Miss Firenze. Two
more were added: Peter Cunningham and Randy.

"Why Randy?" Michael asked.

"It's the name of the young man or boy Cunningham was
calling. Walsh says he didn't mention it to the police which
makes it the kind of thing we're looking for, an omission, a
line of investigation missed or not followed through."

"We don't even have his last name."

"Perhaps Mr. Cunningham will be kind enough to pro-
vide it. Or if he's not kind enough," Howard added grimly,
"perhaps we can see to it that he's scared enough."

"I'm opposed to any kind of force or intimidation,
Howard."

"Are you?"

"I like to think so."

"But not as opposed as you were, say, six months ago."

"No."

"You've changed, Mike. You've changed more than I
have."

"It's a longer fall from a pedestal than from a seat on the
stock exchange. I didn't ask for the pedestal, it simply came
with the territory. I'm glad to be getting free of it."

"What does that mean?"

"I'll go into it another time. Let's get back to work."

They resumed the task they'd started in the late afternoon. Somewhere in the files that Miss Garrison had copied

and delivered to Michael at the church there had to be a list of the clothes found in the closet of the palace, but so far it had not been located. Under clothing there was only a description of what Annamay had been wearing when she left the house with Dru after lunch. There was nothing under apparel, garments, closet, wardrobe, so the clothes in the palace closet were evidently not considered important enough for a separate listing of their own.

A reference was finally located in the report of the sergeant who had first examined the palace after Annamay was reported missing.

Playhouse, clothes closet, contents of:
A child's sweater, green, cardigan style
Two tennis shoes, one white, one blue
A cotton T-shirt
Nylon undershorts, pink
(All the above were identified by Mrs. Chisholm, the housekeeper, as belonging to Annamay Hyatt.)
Two adult evening gowns, one black chiffon, one blue silk, both in need of repair
One black felt hat trimmed with a pink rose
(These clothes were identified by Mrs. Chisholm as having belonged to Kathleen Hyatt, Annamay's mother, and given to the child to play grown-up.)

There was no mention of the high-heeled sandals with the rhinestone straps.

Chapter EIGHT

Dru's report card for the fall semester was sent to her mother by registered mail, not brought home by Dru herself. This was unusual enough. The contents of the enclosed letter were even more unusual:

Dear Mrs. Campbell:

Our efforts to reach you via messages hand-carried by Dru have been unsuccessful. I am therefore using this means of contacting you in regard to the changes in Dru's behavior and grade-point average.

The entire student body was, of course, shocked by the death of Annamay Hyatt and we had to deal with a number of behavioral problems as a consequence. The shock has gradually worn off and the children have returned more or less to normal. The reverse has been the case with Dru. She appeared quite calm in the beginning, almost as if she believed a great fuss was being made over nothing and her cousin would reappear any day unharmed.

Dru, a bright and motivated student, has become more and more inattentive in class, and aggressive to the point of hostility during game time. She has also violated several of the school rules such as using obscene language, smoking in the lavatory and truancy. These things simply do not add up to the Dru we have known since kindergarten.

I feel that you and I had better discuss the situation and see what can be done to help the child.

Yours most sincerely,
Isabelle G. Thomson

Vicki read the letter twice and glanced briefly and reluctantly at the report card. Then she called her husband, John Campbell, at the Museum of Natural History where he worked and told him to come home immediately because something terrible had happened.

John arrived within ten minutes, expecting to find the house in flames, flooded by a broken water pipe, or at least burglarized. Instead he found Vicki sitting at the bar in the lanai drinking a gin and tonic.

He said, "Well?"

"Dru got a C-minus in social studies."

"I am staggered. Appalled. Stunned. Now do you mind if I go back to work? I was in the middle of a meeting."

"By all means go back to your meeting. But I bet if Dru were your *own* daughter you wouldn't object to spending some of your time on her problems."

"Dru isn't my own flesh and blood but I consider her my daughter."

"Then take a look at this." Vicki spread the report card and the letter from the teacher on the bar. "Nothing higher than a C except in science and that was the silkworm project you helped her with. And read what that bitchy woman has to say about Dru's behavior. I haven't noticed any change in her at all."

"I have."

"Then why didn't you say so?"

"I'm saying so now." John put on his reading glasses and studied the report card carefully. "What's all the commotion about? This isn't so bad."

"She used to be an all-A student."

"So this semester she isn't. Maybe she won't be again for some time: Give her a chance to recover. The kid's had a real shaking up. Annamay was her best friend as well as her cousin."

"This may sound silly to you because you're a man and you wouldn't understand. But I wonder if Dru has suddenly realized she's not pretty. It's a terrible disadvantage to a girl not to be pretty."

"How would you know?"

She looked at him suspiciously. "I suppose that was intended as a compliment. Well, I'm not in the mood for compliments. I want to be serious. . . . Next summer we can start having her overbite corrected and eventually something can be done about her nose. But she has those big ears like Gerald and she's going to be too tall."

"Gerald's big ears didn't prevent you from marrying him," John said. "Why did you marry him, by the way?"

"I can't remember."

"Will you be saying that about me someday?"

"Maybe, unless you start taking me seriously. Dru's slipping grades may not be a catastrophe to you. But she simply *has* to be bright if she's not pretty. What a shame she didn't take after my side of the family."

"You should have thought of that when you were rolling in the hay with Mr. Big Ears."

"That was vulgar and uncalled for."

"You asked for it. You know I don't like to hear references to Gerald or any other of your previous liaisons or whatever you call them."

"Lovers."

"Okay, lovers."

"Gerald had a perfectly beautiful build, if you want the truth."

"Spare me a description of his build, ears or any other part of his anatomy, and let's get back to the subject. You dragged me out of an important meeting in order to discuss Dru's problems. So discuss. All you've managed to suggest so far is that it's a shame she didn't take after your side of the family."

"Well, it is a shame, dammit. Annamay looked so much like Kay and me and Dru had to take after—"

"I know, I know. Mr. Big Ears."

"Even Gerald acknowledges the resemblance and he never notices anything unless it's right under his nose. He wears glasses. Poor Dru, maybe she'll have to wear glasses as she gets older. That would be the final straw."

"I wear glasses."

"Only to read with. Gerald wears them to see everything, mostly women. Maybe that's why he prefers big women, they're easier to see."

"If Big Ears had so many faults I don't understand how he could have snagged a perfect jewel like you."

"Now you're getting nasty."

"No, no. Just curious. How did he?"

"He lied a lot."

"And?"

"I believed him. I've always been gullible. I believe everything a person tells me, and it's such a shock when I'm let down, especially by my own daughter."

"What does that mean?"

"Dru has been lying to me lately. Nothing too serious, not yet anyway. But it worries me. She told me the other day she was going over to Heather Park's house after school. I happened to meet Heather and her aunt at the Carlton Plaza that afternoon and Dru wasn't with them. She's becoming secretive. A ten-year-old should have no secrets from her mother."

"That depends on the ten-year-old," John said. "And the mother."

"Annamay was so different. Open, direct. You always knew what she was thinking."

"Annamay is dead. Dru is alive. Comparing the two girls is pointless and destructive. Stop doing it."

"Is that an order?"

"You got it."

She looked ready to cry, then thought better of it and

made herself another drink instead. She didn't offer him one. "All right, you're so clever, Johnny, you handle things. She'll be home in a few minutes. Talk to her."

"Maybe I will," John said. "Or maybe I'll let her talk to me."

"That sounds cool and sweet and reasonable, so try it. Let her talk. The silence will be deafening. She doesn't communicate anymore."

"She might need a new communicatee. I offer my services."

"What she very likely needs is professional help. I'm thinking of setting up an appointment with that new kiddie shrink Sarah Fitzroy takes all her kids to."

"No."

"What do you mean, no?"

"She's too young to start the shrink routine. Lay off her, Vicki. She's going through a phase called growing up."

"She's growing away, not up. And whether she'll be sent to a shrink or not will have to be my decision. She's my daughter."

"She's mine too, and I like her the way she is, without the services of a shrink, plastic surgeon or orthodontist."

He waited for her on the south patio which was sheltered from the wind by a six-foot fence of redwood half-rounds. The fence had been built by Vicki's first husband and it was the only reference she ever made to him. ("That damn fence is beginning to list. Wilbur said it would last forever." "Don't blame Wilbur," John said. "The trunk of the elephant's-foot yucca is pressing against the fence. It will have to be replaced eventually.")

John glanced now at the fence and saw that it was listing another two or three degrees. Replacing it would be an expensive project because the cost of redwood half-rounds had risen astronomically.

He sat down on the glider and began rocking back and

forth until the movement made him a little dizzy. In spite of his confident manner in front of Vicki he felt uneasy, not sure how to approach the problem of Dru's report card. He'd had considerable experience with children of all ages but it was in a professional way. Children were mostly on their best behavior when they were taking part in field trips to the museum itself or to the beaches to observe tide pools or the sloughs to observe sea- and shorebirds. His first close contact with a child was with Dru when he married her mother. She was only nine years old at the time but she treated him like an equal and he found himself treating her the same way. Serious opinions were exchanged, especially at breakfast which they took turns making because Vicki liked to sleep late and the cook didn't arrive until eleven. They were, John believed, friends.

It was nearly three o'clock when he heard the school bus shriek to a stop at the end of the driveway and unload more of its wild cargo.

She didn't look wild. She wore the neat school uniform, dark green jumper with matching sweater and white blouse, and her long brown hair was tied back with a green ribbon. She was carrying a backpack on her shoulder and a striped orange kitten in her arms.

"Hi," John said.

"Hi."

"Who's your friend?"

"A cat."

"Boy or girl?"

"Girl, I think. It's hard to tell with kittens. Do you think you could tell?"

"I can try."

The kitten, not without protest, changed hands.

"It's a boy," John said. "And he's hungry. Better get some milk out of the refrigerator and add a little warm water."

It didn't seem the proper way to begin a discussion of report cards but there wasn't much he could do about it. He held the kitten against his shoulder until Dru returned with a bowl of milk. They both watched as the kitten lapped at the milk with his tiny pink tongue.

"He's very cute," Dru said. "Don't you think?"

"Very. But you shouldn't pick up strays."

"I didn't. I won him, fair and square."

"Where?"

"At school."

"Do they hold raffles there these days?"

"No. Kristy Dougherty's mother brought them to school in a basket and she offered them to the students who thought of the cleverest names. So I suggested Marmalady and I won first choice. Now I can't use it being as he's not a lady. Would you like me to call him John after you?"

"Maybe you'd better not name him at all until you make certain he's going to be staying."

"He's got to stay. He's mine. I won him."

"What if your mother—?"

"She can't take him away from me. He's mine. I won him fair and square."

What wasn't fair and square, in John's opinion, was Mrs. Dougherty's method of getting rid of a litter of kittens, but this was hardly the time for a discussion of ethics. Dru was crouched protectively over the kitten while it continued to drink.

"Dru, listen a minute."

"I won him fair and square," she repeated. "If he can't stay I won't either. I'll run away like Annamay and everyone will think I'm dead and have a funeral for me and they'll all be crying and *I'll* be laughing."

"Is this what you really think, that Annamay is alive somewhere and laughing?"

She gave no indication that she had heard the question.

"You went to her funeral, Dru. You saw Annamay's coffin."

"Maybe she wasn't in it. There were just a bunch of

bones. One of the girls at school said they could have been animal bones."

"They weren't animal bones, they were Annamay's."

"No one ever proved it. They didn't have her name printed on them and there were no distinguished marks."

"There were no distinguishing marks, no. But the coroner's jury—"

"They were only people. People make mistakes all the time."

He knelt on the flagstones beside her and began stroking her hair the way she was stroking the kitten. "Listen to me, Dru. It would be nice to think that Annamay is alive somewhere but it simply isn't so."

"One of the girls in Bible study said that only very good people die young. Annamay wasn't that good. *She just wasn't that good.*"

"You're going to be hearing many things throughout your life. You'll have to decide what's reasonable and what isn't. I have no doubt you can do it. You're a bright girl."

"No one else thinks so."

"Everyone thinks so."

"No, they don't. I got a bad report card this semester. I know because when they were handing out the reports on Wednesday only two of us didn't get ours, me and Mary Jo, and Mary Jo is the class ass."

"I have your report card in my pocket," John said. "Want to see it?"

She shook her head.

"Oh, come on, have a look. It's not so bad. I've seen worse. In fact, I've had worse."

"Not really."

"Scout's honor. Now let's sit down at the table, you and I and the marmalade man, and study the report card and see what's the matter."

"What's the matter is the teacher doesn't like me."

"That could be a factor but probably not a very big one."

"If the good die young she's going to live forever," Dru said. "The kids all call her Dragon Lady."

"What do you call her?"

"In front of her or behind her?"

"In front of her will do for starters."

"Isabelle."

"You address her as Isabelle?"

"Yes."

"Why?"

"I like to see her face get all red. It's very interesting. The red begins at the neck and climbs up until even the tip of her nose is as pink as a bunny's."

"Oh Lord," John said. "Holy cats."

"It's a good clean scientific experiment, *I* think."

"Obviously Miss Thomson doesn't agree."

"She has no sense of humor."

"I'm losing mine in a hurry. Come on." He helped her to her feet and they sat down at the round glass table with the report card and the kitten in front of them.

"You're an excellent reader," John said. "Why the C in English?"

"Isabelle—"

"Miss Thomson."

"Miss Thomson wants me to read what she wants me to read and I want to read what I want to read."

"I'm afraid I'll have to take Miss Thomson's side on that one. It's her job to educate the students, not vice versa."

"A little vice versa doesn't hurt."

"Not every teacher appreciates vice versas, Miss Thomson being one of them. And frankly, I'm beginning to have considerable sympathy for the woman."

"Grown-ups always take each other's side."

"Look at the facts, Dru. You haven't done the required reading and you've been behaving toward the teachers in an insolent manner. Is that a fair statement?"

"It's true but it's not fair because it doesn't include how funny she looks when her face gets red, and also how she has no sense of humor."

"It includes your being a pain in the neck in class. You've been deliberately causing trouble, haven't you?"

"Yes."

"Why?"

"I don't know. I guess because it's fun."

"For a girl who's having fun you don't appear very happy."

"What does everyone expect me to do, go around laughing all the time and getting A's on my report card and looking like a movie star?"

"I don't expect—"

"Mom does. She expects me to be even perfecter than Annamay." She took the ribbon out of her hair and tied it around the kitten's neck. He was too drowsy to protest and went to sleep in the crook of her arm. "If she doesn't let me keep him I'm going to tell on her. There are plenty of things you don't know."

"And don't want to hear."

"Like how she was so disappointed when I was born that she had herself fixed so she wouldn't have any more children."

"That's not the reason she did it. What gave you that idea?"

"I figured it out."

"You figured wrong. The doctors advised her against any more pregnancies."

"Oh bull. She just didn't want any more like *me*. Well, I don't care. Little brothers and sisters are a nuisance anyway. I'd rather have a cat." She pressed her cheek against the kitten's head. "Do you suppose when he wakes up and finds himself wearing a ribbon he'll feel silly?"

"More likely he'll be frightened."

"And maybe run away?"

"Maybe."

"I'll take it right off." She removed the ribbon so gently the kitten barely stirred. "You like him too, don't you, John?"

"Oh yes. Very much."

"Then it's you and me against her if she says no. And two yeses count more than one no. That's simple arithmetic. So we win. Say it, John. *We win.* Please."

"It won't do much good to say it. We've got to try a little psychology. How about telling her you won a horse? Then she might be quite happy to settle for a kitten."

"That's awfully clever."

"Thank you."

"A grown-up horse or a pony?"

"A grown-up might have greater shock value."

She let out a small giggle, then immediately became sober again. "John, do you think a person's true character shows in her face?"

"No."

"It could be true anyway. And if it is, which do you suppose causes which? Is the character there first and then you get your face from that? Or is your face first and that causes your character?"

"Physical features are inherited. Character is also inherited but is more subject to environmental influences. That's my opinion."

Dru thought this over carefully, then closed her eyes. "What color are my eyes?"

"Is this a new game?"

"What color?"

"Blue," he said. "Blue-ish."

"They're green. Ugly mean green with brown specks in them. Also they're small."

"No, they're not."

"I have small mean green eyes," Dru said grimly. "Now

what if you met two girls and one of them had big blue eyes and the other had small ugly greens, which one would you want for a daughter?"

"The heck with both of them. I pick you."

"Not really."

"Scout's honor. Gaze into my small ugly browns and see if I'm telling the truth."

"You can be terribly silly sometimes. You don't have brown eyes. They're blue."

"That's to fool people so they won't suspect I have an ugly brown character."

"You don't have an ugly brown character either."

"Sure I do. Brown with a spot of black here and there, traces of purple, a few patches of gray. Boy, am I a mess."

She looked at him severely. "I think you should treat me more like an adult."

"Okay, Miss Adult. Here's your report card. Take it and study it. And this semester cut out the smartassing and get down to business."

Vicki had come out of the house and was crossing the patio, her heels making peevish little taps on the flagstones. She was obviously perturbed because she didn't even notice the kitten, or at least pretended she didn't.

"Mr. Hyatt, Howard's father, is here and wants to see Dru. I'm not sure what he has in mind but it might be connected with Annamay's palace."

"I don't know anything about it," Dru said.

"Tell him that."

"He won't believe me."

"Go and talk to him anyway, dammit. I can't have him parked outside the front door for the rest of the day."

"I don't want to."

"*Go.* You hear me?"

The kitten, disturbed by the noise, woke up and meowed. Dru quickly transferred him to John's arms, whispered, "Two against one," and ran around the side of the house.

Mr. Hyatt's dignified black Cadillac was parked in the semi-circular driveway and Mr. Hyatt was standing beside it polishing the rear-view mirror with his handkerchief. When he saw Dru coming toward him he put the handkerchief back in his pocket and acknowledged the child's presence with a courteous little nod of his head.

Neither of them spoke for a long time. Then Dru said, "I won a cat."

"That's nice. It's always pleasant to win something, especially a cat."

"Right now it's only a kitten. But someday it will be a cat."

"All the better. You will have the joy of watching it grow up. Watching young creatures grow up has been one of the greatest pleasures of my life." There was another silence, this one broken by the old man. "Annamay didn't make it."

"Mr. Hyatt—"

"What a pity. She would have become a lovely woman and borne beautiful children."

"Not necessarily," Dru said. "My mother used to be a lovely woman and *she* had *me*. A lot depends on the man."

"Annamay might one day have married a real prince and lived in a real palace."

"No, sir. She was going to marry Ben and he's just an architect and lives in a crummy apartment down by the harbor, my mother says."

"Annamay marry Ben? Dear me, no. He would never have waited for her. He's quite ready for matrimony right now."

"I know. He's got women stashed all over town."

"He does?"

"Yes, sir."

"Who told you that?"

"My mother."

"Then it's probably correct."

"Probably. She gets the dirt on everyone."

"I see." He stared up at the sky, blinked, wiped his eyes on the same handkerchief he'd used to clean the car's rearview mirror. "And do you also admire Ben?"

"Oh sure. He's like an uncle. I've had a whole string of uncles and Ben is more fun than any of them." Dru paused, frowning. "Do you know what a funny uncle is?"

"I don't believe I've heard the expression, no."

"My friend Connie at school has one but she won't talk about it. She just squizzles up her mouth and rolls her eyes. She always has tons of money to spend. She's fourteen and goes steady and keeps a bottle of booze in her locker."

"Booze?"

"Vodka."

"Perhaps she simply fills an empty vodka bottle with water and keeps it in her locker to show off."

"No. I tried some. It burned my throat. I'll be going steady myself pretty soon. I like a boy called Kevin. He's twelve and plays soccer and intends to be a mountain climber. He practices by climbing trees."

"Do you like to climb trees also?"

Her face reddened and she crossed her arms on her chest as if to defend herself against an attack. "No. It makes you dizzy looking down." She closed her eyes to such narrow slits that she could barely see Mr. Hyatt's polished boots and the stain on her skirt where the kitten had dribbled milk. "I hate looking down from high places. Annamay and me, we never climbed trees, *ever*. . . . I'd like to go now and look after my cat."

"In a minute," Mr. Hyatt said quietly. "Why are you nervous, Dru?"

"My cat needs me. And I hate thinking of looking down."

"Then look up. There's a bird in the oak tree over there, quite a large bird with beautiful blue feathers. What do you suppose it is?"

"I don't suppose. I *know* what it is. A scrub jay. John tells me all about birds." She sounded weary. "In addition to all the things I have to learn in school John makes me memorize birds and trees and flowers and rocks. Probably stars are next."

"Stars will be good for you. You always have to look up for stars."

Dru looked up, seeing only a watery sun half-hidden in a cloud bank. "There aren't any stars."

"There will be later."

"Not tonight. It's too foggy."

"They will be there even if you don't see them."

"What's the use of that, I'd like to know."

For reasons he didn't understand, she seemed to need comforting and he attempted to put a soothing hand on her shoulder, but she ducked out of reach. "I've got to go now and tend to my cat."

"Let me touch you, child. I mean you no harm."

"I'm not supposed to be touched by strangers."

"Strangers? Why, I'm Annamay's grandfather and you are her cousin and her very best friend."

"Best. Not very best."

"You shared each other's secrets," he said. "Didn't you?"

"I guess so. Some."

"And she showed you where there was a key to the palace door?"

"Yes, because I often left things inside and had to go back and get them and sometimes she wouldn't be there to let me in."

"And did you inform other people about the key?"

"No, sir. But *she* probably did. She was such a baby. She couldn't keep secrets to herself, she always had to blab. She even told Kevin I loved him and he got shy and wouldn't even look at me for ages."

Again the old man wiped his eyes on the soiled handkerchief. "It was a mistake, that palace. Having a place of their

140

own permits children to get into trouble. They need supervision."

"We didn't get into trouble. We didn't do anything bad there."

"It was a mistake. I gave Howard and Kay my opinion at the very beginning, but they were carried away by Ben's ideas. He was so enthusiastic about it he was like a child himself. He built that palace for *him,* not for Annamay."

"You can't blame the palace for everything."

"Children cannot handle such freedoms. They do things that—"

"She didn't die in the palace," Dru said roughly. "She isn't even dead. She got up and walked away and she's hiding somewhere, laughing at you grown-ups for burying a bunch of old animal bones."

"Do you think she'll be coming back?"

"Eventually. When she feels like it."

"You believe that, Dru?"

"I said it, didn't I?"

"But do you believe it?"

"It's true. I don't care what anyone else thinks, it's true."

A pair of tears squeezed out of his eyes and crawled down the crevices of his face. "You are deluded, Dru. You are a sick little girl."

"And you're a crazy old man."

"Please don't scream like that."

"You're a crazy old man. And I'm going to tell everyone you wanted me to take off my clothes and you offered to give me money. Only I wouldn't take it because I don't do bad things."

"You wouldn't tell such cruel lies."

"Why not? You're just a crazy old man and I hate you. I hate all of you."

He watched her run up the front steps and into the house. Then he got back behind the wheel of his car and sat there motionless for a long time. His tears had turned to stone, leaving a terrible ache inside his eyes.

"She didn't die. . . . She got up and walked away and she's hiding somewhere, laughing at you grown-ups for burying a bunch of old animal bones."

Chapter NINE

Mr. Cassandra had finished work for the day. He left his tambourine and robe in his hotel room and went down to the bar on the ground floor where he held court nearly every evening. It wasn't much of a court, eight stools and a young bartender who went to school during the day and yawned a great deal at night.

Mr. Cassandra drank only on special occasions. But using both his prolific memory and his imagination, he could think of special occasions at the drop of a hat: Presidents' birthdays, the ends of wars, the completion of dams, bridges and tall buildings, the first Mardi Gras, the invention of the wheel, the Bill of Rights and Fridays, all of these deserved to be celebrated, and were.

The clientele of the bar was mixed, but they all had one thing in common: None of them could shut Mr. Cassandra up.

"Many, many times throughout my life I could have made me a fortune. And every time I blew it. I blew it again this week. I had something valuable to sell and instead of selling it I gave it away. And what is this something? you ask."

"I didn't ask," said the man sitting beside him. "Nobody asked. Nobody wants to—"

"A name. Simply a name, that's all. Randy. Know whose name that is? A chicken's."

"Where the hell you coming from, man? You ain't got no chickens. The hotel don't allow pets."

Mr. Cassandra continued, unruffled. "At a certain time on a certain day this man Cunningham was at a certain place calling for Randy. He told the police he was calling his cat. Cat, my ass. He was calling one of his chickens who'd flown the coop. What I should have done is gone to Cunningham and told him I was willing to forget the whole incident in return for a nice sum of money. And why didn't I? you ask."

"I didn't ask. I don't give a shit."

"Because I'm an honest man, that's why. Honesty is the family curse. I had an uncle who forgot to pay his income taxes for a few years and when the IRS caught up with him they asked him point-blank if he'd paid his taxes during that time and he said no. They sent him to the slammer for two years."

"Man, he must of got up front of some mean dude of a judge."

"He should have pleaded not guilty but the family curse was on him. A lie would have caught in his throat like a fishbone, would have clutched his stomach like an iron claw."

"Then how come he cheat on his taxes?"

"He didn't cheat. It was an honest mistake."

Such honesty deserved to be commemorated. A round of drinks was paid for by Mr. Cassandra who suddenly remembered that that very day was the anniversary of his uncle's release from the slammer.

The curiosity of the young bartender, ordinarily dulled by fatigue, was roused at the idea of a chicken called Randy who was worth a fortune.

"He had no feathers," Mr. Cassandra explained.

"I got a friend who owned a real old canary that hardly had any feathers left. No feathers, couldn't sing, couldn't fly. . . . If this guy Cunningham is so rich, how come he keeps chickens?"

144

"To keep the kind of chickens he keeps and stay clear of the police, you have to be rich. Real rich."

"How'd he get that rich?"

"He had a mother," Mr. Cassandra said.

As soon as she opened the door Michael recognized her as the overweight overdressed woman he'd noticed at Annamay's funeral services. She had sat in the back row between Ben York and a handsome middle-aged man with bronze skin and silvery hair. The strangers were later identified to him as Mrs. Cunningham and her son, Peter.

She wore the same kind of costume she'd worn at the funeral services, layers of a gauzy material that drew attention to her weight instead of camouflaging it, just as the heavy makeup drew attention to her wrinkles instead of hiding them. She was, Michael guessed, about seventy. In the police file Cunningham was listed as fifty-one. His mother had not revealed her age.

Michael said, "Mrs. Cunningham?"

"Yes." She peered up at him, blinking her eyes rapidly to clarify his image and her memory. "Do I know you?"

"We haven't met formally. I'm Michael Dunlop."

"Oh dear me. The minister?"

"Yes."

"How odd." She leaned heavily against one side of the doorframe as if she needed help in supporting the weight of heaven as well as her own. "Unless of course you're collecting for something?"

"No. At least not money. Let's consider this a social call."

"I can't imagine why a minister would pay a social call on me. Unless Peter put you up to it. He has quite a nasty sense of humor like his father."

"I'm not acquainted with your son."

"Oh."

"May I come in?"

"I suppose. If you're quite sure you're not an impostor."

"I'm quite sure." *Not entirely,* he thought, and wondered if Mrs. Cunningham was especially perceptive or a good guesser.

Everything in the massive old house seemed to be made of wood, paneled walls, beamed ceiling, parquet floor. In the living room where she led him, the most imposing piece of furniture was a concert-sized grand piano made of rosewood which was no longer used for pianos, and bearing the name of a manufacturer who had gone out of business years ago. The lid was open and the keyboard exposed as if someone might have been interrupted while playing it. But the bench and keys were dusty and there was no music in sight.

She saw him looking at the piano and said with a sigh, "My son, Peter, is the musician of the family. Not a very good one, I'm afraid. He plays extra loudly to cover his mistakes but somehow one hears them anyway. The house is what Peter's friends call live."

"Because of all the wood."

"Yes. Sounds travel to every nook and cranny. There's no escaping Peter's mistakes." She let out a small snort of amusement but suppressed it so quickly Michael wasn't positive he'd heard it. "When Peter played Bach's *Well-Tempered Clavichord* my late husband used to call it the *Ill-Tempered Clavichord.* . . . Will you sit down?"

"Thanks."

"Now what's the protocol? Do I offer you a drink or something like that?"

"It's not necessary."

"I intend to have a drop or two myself so perhaps you will join me."

She produced a bottle of cheap scotch and a yellow plastic tumbler from behind a boxed set of Shakespeare's comedies. The set still wore the publisher's transparent wrapping but the bottle was more than half empty.

"There's only one glass so we shall have to take turns.

146

Peter keeps all the good booze and crystal locked up when he's away."

Half a dozen questions rose to the surface of Michael's mind: How far away is he? Out of town? Out of state? When did he leave? When will he be back? Who is Randy? But he said only, "Taking turns will be fine."

"I could ring for another glass but the maid is watching television while she irons and even if she heard the bell she'd be terribly annoyed and pretend she doesn't speak English. According to Peter, I don't know how to handle the Mexican servants. His method is to use nouns and act out the verbs. What method do you use?"

"I speak Spanish." *It beats acting out the verbs.* "I had a parish in East L.A. for a while. It's now part of a shopping mall."

"I have no trouble communicating with our houseboy. He's an Indian, the kind from India who meditates. His English is perfect. He's on vacation right now." She poured a liberal amount of scotch into the plastic tumbler and handed it to him. "Here. You first."

The liquid had the smell and sting of carbolic acid and the first mouthful was hard to swallow. The second was only a little easier.

Her snort this time was unmistakable. "Not very good, is it? But then one doesn't drink the stuff for taste. One drinks it for anxiety, insomnia, high blood pressure, fibrillation, despair. Do you have any of those?"

"Not regularly."

"But sometimes?"

"Yes."

"Which one? I mean, which one do you have the oftenest?"

"Despair, I suppose."

"And you're a minister?"

"Yes."

"How odd." She poured the rest of the bottle of scotch into the plastic tumbler. "One doesn't expect *ministers* to suffer from despair. After all, they have a nice safe forever in store for them."

"Do they?"

"If *they* don't, who does?"

"That's a question I can't answer."

She didn't say, "How odd," again but she looked as if she were thinking it. "I'm disappointed. I always thought if I managed to get through this life, something better was waiting for me. If there's not, then this is all, this is it?"

"Perhaps."

"What a dreadful prospect."

"Sorry."

"In fact I find the whole conversation extremely depressing."

"Sorry about that too."

"Ministers should say encouraging things like how everybody will get their reward in heaven. Don't you believe that?"

"No."

"You must have believed it once or you wouldn't have become a minister."

"I believed it once."

"What happened?"

"A little girl died."

"Is that all?"

"There were other things as well but that was the main one."

The liquor was already having its effect. Mrs. Cunningham's face seemed to be coming apart, melting like gelatin and held together only by the thick crust of makeup. One of her eyes had gone slightly out of focus, making her look a little like Annamay's doll, Marietta, with her permanent strabismus.

"There must be a heaven," she said. "There must be. Otherwise how could I endure all this—all this—"

She stared around the room with a kind of desperation, and Michael wondered what it was she couldn't endure: the house? the furnishings? Peter's mistakes on the piano?

"All this what, Mrs. Cunningham?"

"Sometimes it's not nice living here," she said vaguely. "But I have no other place to go. Peter says I wouldn't be tolerated anywhere else. So he lets me stay here and he has promised never to leave me because then I would be alone. I couldn't bear being alone. So like it or not, I must put up with his friends, smile at their stupid antics, pretend not to mind when they leave their smelly clothes all over the house, yes, sometimes even draped on my piano, my beloved piano."

"It's an antique, I see."

"It belonged to my grandfather. He gave it to me when I was in my teens and studying music quite seriously. I don't play anymore except at Christmas a few carols when I think no one is listening. 'Silent Night,' 'Come, All Ye Faithful,' 'Hark! the Herald Angels Sing.'" She reached out suddenly and grabbed his coat sleeve. "There must be angels. Surely there must be angels."

"If you want to believe—"

"No no. *Tell* me. Tell me there are angels."

"All right," he said heavily. "There are angels."

"Who are looking out for me."

"Who are looking out for you."

"I can't live without angels."

She sat down on the piano bench and played the opening bars of "The First Noel," singing the words in a thin sweet soprano. Listening to her Michael thought, *She's right, of course. There must be angels. People had to have them.*

She played badly and she knew it. "I've lost my touch. Grandfather would be disappointed at hearing such sounds coming from his cherished piano. Thank God he can't hear the way Peter's friends bang on it. 'Chopsticks.' Isn't it funny, children are still playing 'Chopsticks' the way they did in my youth."

"You speak of Peter's friends as children," Michael said. "How old are they?"

"I don't ask. In this house nobody dares to refer to age. Peter can't stand the idea of growing old. When he started getting bald at an early age I often heard him sobbing in his room at night. You look surprised. Didn't you know he is bald?"

"No."

"Bald as an egg. All that lovely silvery hair, not a strand of it is real. He began buying wigs before he was thirty, brown at first, then each succeeding one a little grayer until they were entirely gray like those he wears now. He kept every one of them. They're on wig stands in his bedroom. It's spooky, all those rows of heads staring at you without eyes. Poor Peter, he likes to think his little friends don't know he wears a wig. How silly. It's almost impossible to fool a child. Don't you agree?"

"Yes," Michael said.

Yet someone had fooled Annamay. She and Dru had left the Hyatt house together and gone down to the creek in search of polliwogs. When they didn't find any, Dru lost interest and went on home. What then? Where were the dogs?

"We left them at home," Dru had told the coroner's jury, *"because they always waded in the water and scared creatures away."*

If the dogs had been present, what creatures might they have scared away? A con man with a tambourine? A mad old madam on one of her escapades? A chicken hawk looking for one of his chickens? Someone nobody had even thought of?

"Peter's friends," Michael said, "Who are they?"

"Nobody. Riffraff. He picks them up off the street and

after they've eaten our food and drunk our booze and stolen whatever they can get their hands on, they return to the street."

"Are any of them girls?"

"Girls?" She stood up, swaying slightly as if the floor had begun crumbling under her feet. "Of course not. Peter isn't interested in girls. He promised me when he was in his early teens that he would never marry, never leave me alone."

"I meant little girls." He wondered how far he could go without pushing her over the brink. "Like Annamay Hyatt."

"Are you implying—? Yes, I see you are. Well, you couldn't be more mistaken. Peter hadn't the faintest interest in little girls, especially the Hyatt child."

"Why especially, Mrs. Cunningham?"

"She was a sneaky devil, always creeping up on him and spying. She and that friend of hers spied on nearly everyone in the neighborhood, peering over walls and through fences." She had begun swaying again, rhythmically, like a distraught mother rocking a sick child. "My son was not interested in girls. Any girls, of any age. He promised me he would never get married and leave me here alone."

"I'm sure he never will."

"I— You're very kind." She dabbed at her eyes with a handkerchief. They were as tearless as the wig stands in Peter's bedroom. "Oh, I'm glad Peter isn't here. He hates me to become emotional like this."

"Where is he, Mrs. Cunningham?"

"San Francisco. He took Randy along to look after his clothes and things."

"Randy is his special friend?"

"Oh no. He's our houseboy. He's an Indian. From India, I mean. He meditates."

"The servants of all the families in the neighborhood were questioned by the police. No one by the name of Randy appears in the files."

"His real name is Maharandhi Rau. He was questioned

by the police several times but of course he didn't know anything. On the afternoon the Hyatt girl disappeared Randy was down in the citrus grove meditating, and when he meditates he can't see or hear anything at all. He's on a different plane, in another dimension." She sounded wistful, as if other places, other times were more appealing than here and now. "I wonder if meditation would do me any good."

"It wouldn't hurt to try it."

"I suppose one has to select a subject to meditate about."

"Probably."

"Very well, I choose angels."

"That's an interesting choice."

"I shall start immediately.... That is, as soon as you leave."

"I was on the point of leaving."

"How nice of you to suggest meditating. When Randy gets home he'll be terribly surprised to find he's not the only one who can reach a different plane in another dimension. There *I'll* be, waiting for him."

"He'll be surprised, all right."

"What a joke on him. Ho ho ho."

Santa Claus couldn't have said it better.

Her mood had taken a sharp upswing and pulled her body along with it. She held herself erect and steady and the hand she offered him was firm, her smile gracious.

"I've enjoyed our little visit, Mr. Dunlop. Do come again."

"I'll try." Ho ho ho.

Howard, who started his working hours at six in the morning when the New York Stock Exchange opened, left the office at two and was back at the guest cottage by two-thirty. He found Michael waiting for him.

"We can scratch Randy's name off the list," Michael said.

"Why?"

"He was questioned by the police several times under his

152

real name, Maharandhi Rau. I've just finished going over the report. Here, read the conclusion of the last tape for yourself."

"All right."

DEPUTY DE SALLE:

So you were meditating, Mr. Rau, down in the citrus grove. For how long?

RAU:

Who knows? Time is meaningless. I am into forever.

DEPUTY DE SALLE:

I'm on an eight-hour shift myself so I got to watch the clock. How long, Mr. Rau?

RAU:

Until I heard voices penetrating my ears and felt my soul returning to this dimension.

DEPUTY DE SALLE:

So what happened in this dimension?

RAU:

I went back to the house and played gin rummy with the old lady. Allah frowns on such frivolity. When I pick up the cards he averts his face. Either my luck is astonishingly bad or else she reads my mind. I owe her nearly three and a half million dollars.

DEPUTY DE SALLE:

Don't sweat it. You got a long time to pay if you're into forever. Whose voices penetrated your ears?

RAU:

I was being summoned by my master.

DEPUTY DE SALLE:

Why?

RAU:

To play gin with his old lady. She was bugging him.

DEPUTY DE SALLE:

You didn't see two little girls down by the creek?

RAU:

No girls, no boys, no humans at all. I was alone in the universe.

DEPUTY DE SALLE:

Thank you, Mr. Rau. I'll see you at another time.

RAU:

Almost certainly. Everyone meets again. That is why we must never do evil. Those to whom evil is done do evil in return even if it takes several thousand years.

DEPUTY DE SALLE:

I'll try to remember that.

RAU:

You will be wise to do so.

"All right," Howard said, putting the typed page back on the table. "Scratch Randy. Who's next?"

"Nobody. His was the last name on the list."

"So where do we go from here? Dozens of questions remain unanswered For instance, why wasn't she found sooner?"

"That question has been raised by a number of people, in newspaper editorials, letters to the editor, interviews with elected officials. A variety of reasons have been given, some conjectural, some scientific. First, there were too many volunteers in the field. Most of them genuinely wanted to help, some simply wanted to be heroes, a few had their eyes on the reward money. But they all had one thing in common: They were untrained, didn't know what to look for or how to look for it. Their presence also disturbed the tracking dogs who were brought in, though there were also other factors involving the dogs. Many species of wildlife still roam the area, especially nocturnal ones who are attracted by the avocado and citrus groves—possums, raccoons, wood rats, skunks. One spray of a skunk can cover all other odors for some time."

"I know." Howard recalled the occasion when Newf decided to challenge a skunk. The battle was lost before it even began. A hurried call to a veterinarian revealed the fact that no progress had been made in dealing with the problem and the solution was the same as it was in Howard's childhood. The dog had to be soaked in tomato juice and then shampooed. Newf's hundred and seventy pounds were covered by thick hair from two to four inches long and the treatment was slow and difficult. But eventually, after the application of a dozen giant cans of tomato juice, all of Kay's shampoo, Howard's aftershave lotion, Chizzy's perfume and two blow dryers, Newf was anxious to resume his role of family dog instead of skunk-fighter. The winner's scent remained on Newf's nose and forehead where he had refused to accept treatment, but Annamay didn't mind. He spent the night in her bedroom.

Chizzy was rather bitter about the perfume. "My brother-in-law gave it to me for Christmas. White Shoulders. He probably paid a fortune for it. He's an electrician."

"I'll buy you a quart of the stuff," Howard said.

Only now did he realize that he'd forgotten to buy it. Tomorrow, he thought. Tomorrow as soon as the stores open.

". . . Are you listening, Howard?"

"Certainly. Go on."

"Another possible reason why the tracking dogs failed was suggested by a botanist. Anise, a perennial weed growing throughout the canyon, was in full bloom at the time. Its odor is short-range but powerful. So much for the dogs, who might simply have been inadequately trained, and back to the people who were not trained at all. Aside from the fact that there were too many amateurs in the field, the nature of another factor must be considered. Annamay was found under a large oak tree whose base was overgrown with poison oak. Now the police are reluctant to admit that their men might have taken pains to avoid or skim over such areas, but they obviously did. It's understandable. Clean-up crews employed by the city and county demand extra pay and protective clothing when they have to work with poison oak. So the police have their answers, the tracking dogs have theirs, and we're left with the questions. Sorry, Howard. It looks like a dead end."

Howard pressed his hands against his temples, moving his head from side to side in agonized denial. "God. God almighty. There must be something we can do."

"I'm afraid not. Sorry."

"Sorry. Yes, everyone's sorry. . . . Leave me alone now, will you, Mike? I want to—have to—don't know, scream, curse, roll on the floor, bang my head against the wall."

"Go easy on yourself, Howard. We did the best we could."

"Which was nothing, absolutely nothing. Now beat it. Please."

Michael hesitated at the door. "God forbid I should interfere with some good old-fashioned head banging but I hate to leave you in a depressed mood. Kay's home. She waved at the window when I drove past the house. Why don't you go over and talk to her?"

"I have nothing to say and neither has she. Put it this way: A volcano erupted in our life and the crater it left is too wide to shout across. So don't try playing marriage counselor or psychiatrist. Don't even try playing minister."

"If you're telling me I'm no good at it, I agree."

"I'm telling you, butt out."

"I'm on my way," Michael said. "And thanks."

"For what?"

"The advice."

"I didn't give you any advice."

"I think you did." *Don't try playing minister. All right, I won't. Now how do I break the news to Lorna?—* "Hey *Lorna, me and God have split." No, make it serious. . . .* "After years of doubt I have decided to quit a profession the basic premise of which I can no longer accept."

As he closed the door behind him he felt no guilt or regret. That would come later, in dreams, on dark winter mornings, sunny afternoons, behind the eyes and inside his stomach, anytime, anyplace. Right now his mind and body were immune. He was free, buoyant and, for a minute or two, happy.

Outside, the late afternoon wind had started blowing in from the sea, cold and wet and timeless. It smelled of the past, flotsam left stranded on the beach at low tide, yet it seemed to promise a future and he felt like breaking into a run, running all the way home.

There was no chance to run. His ancient Buick was waiting at the curb and Howard's father was sitting in the front seat. Mr. Hyatt looked chilled and his voice had a trace of irritability. "Did you know this seat has a broken spring?"

"Yes."

"Are you going to have it fixed or repaired?"

"Probably not."

"I see. You feel the car is too old to merit further attention."

"Not at all. Mr. Hyatt, did you wait for me out here in order to discuss car seats?"

"Oh, no."

"What then?"

"I'm worried. Kay had a phone call and she's crying. Kay doesn't cry anymore, ever. Someone is coming to the house to see her, someone with bad news, someone she's afraid of."

"How do you know this?"

"I was in the upstairs hall when the phone rang in her bedroom and I heard her answer. I don't approve of eavesdropping but it's the only way I get information anymore. I heard her say the name Ben. But it can't be Ben who's coming. She wouldn't cry about that. She likes Ben, he's like a little brother to her. So it can't be Ben who's coming, can it?"

"I don't know."

"What are you going to do about it, Michael?"

"Nothing."

"But—but Kay is crying."

"That's her privilege." *I'm no longer in the ministering business, old man. I was no good at it anyway. Ask my friend Howard, my wife, Lorna.*

The old man's head had sunk down into the collar of his sweater as if the muscles that held it erect had lost their strength. His face had a bluish tinge and his voice shook. "I regret having bothered you."

"You didn't," Michael said. "I'll drive you back to the house."

"No, thank you. I can walk."

He got out of the car, bracing himself against the wind. His trousers twitched and flapped around his legs, outlining his bony knees and sharp shins.

"Mr. Hyatt."

"You go along now, Michael."

"You're forcing me to think you're a stubborn old man."

Mr. Hyatt looked a little startled, then he turned and without another word got back into the car, and sat with his hands folded quietly in his lap.

Michael put the key in the ignition. After a few coughs and wheezes the engine turned over, making the smooth powerful sound of its heyday. Mr. Hyatt listened to it with obvious pleasure, as if he felt the smooth powerful sounds of his own heyday stirring inside him.

"They don't make cars like this anymore."

"No, sir."

"You should really have this seat replaced, Michael."

"I don't have time to scout the junkyards."

"Junkyards? No, no. You must buy a new seat."

"They don't make seats like this anymore either, Mr. Hyatt."

"A pity. The design is good and it's actually quite comfortable except for the broken spring."

"I'll see what I can do about it."

He stopped the car under the portico at the front door of the main house and the old man got out again.

"It would be nice if you came in and talked to Kay, Michael."

"Many things would be nice if." It would be nice if he didn't have to tell Lorna he was leaving the ministry. It would be nice if she didn't scream, didn't remind him what a failure he'd been as a husband, provider, partner, comforter. It would be nice if he could just walk away without saying or hearing anything.

"Kay will be grateful for your interest, Michael," the old man said. "Very grateful."

If Kay was grateful she managed to conceal it nicely. She gave Mr. Hyatt a frown that sent him scurrying off down the hall. Then she turned the frown on Michael.

"I'd ask you to come in but I don't have time to talk right now."

"I'll come in anyway if I may. It's cold out here."

"It won't be much warmer in here, I assure you. But all right. I can't very well turn away a shivering minister, can I?"

"On behalf of my fellow shiverers, thanks."

He followed her into what Kay called her tea room, a small area between the dining room and the kitchen. There was an ornate silver tea service on the teakwood table but the air smelled of coffee.

Her frown had faded somewhat but her voice was still unfriendly. "Did Howard send you?"

"No."

"You simply dropped in on the spur of the moment? I'm not buying that."

"I'm not selling. The reason I'm here is that Mr. Hyatt told me you received a phone call which upset you."

"Upset me? Do I look upset? I'm not one bloody bit upset. And I wish my father-in-law and Chizzy would stop listening in on conversations that are none of their business."

"Everything about you is their business, Kay," Michael said bluntly. "So what happened and who's coming here?"

Instead of answering immediately she sat down at the teakwood table with the silver tea service in front of her like a shield. This was her place and taking it seemed to restore her poise.

"It was a woman," she said. "I've never met her but I know her name, Quinn, and her position in life."

"And what's her position?"

"Horizontal."

"I see."

"Rumor has it she's not a professional, but a very gifted amateur."

"Mr. Hyatt overheard the name Ben. How does Ben fit into this?"

"Snugly. She's his current live-in. I don't know her first name. Ben calls her Quinn and that's how she identified herself on the phone."

"Why does she want to see you, Kay?"

"I'm not sure. She sounded, not drunk exactly, but under the influence of something. She insisted on coming here to see me in person."

"Why?"

"She has something to tell me about Ben." Kay stared out the window with its view of the lily pond and the marble dolphins that kept the water fresh. "I think it concerns Annamay."

"Did she actually say so?"

"She hinted at a close connection between them. Too close."

"She wouldn't be more explicit?"

"Not over the phone.... Annamay and Ben. The two names together always seemed so natural and wholesome.

Now there's this doubt in my mind. I keep thinking of incidents, trying to remember details, wondering if they were as innocent as they appeared."

"Quinn probably intends you to do just that. So don't do it. Don't speculate. Wait until you hear some facts if she has any. She may simply be a troubled woman, jealous of Ben's friends and trying to alienate them."

"Not them," Kay said. "Me. She thinks I'm the Other Woman in her love life."

"Do you want me to stay with you?"

"No."

"I'll be at home. Call me there if you need anything."

"Thank you, Michael."

They shook hands formally and briefly. She had regained control of herself and he was pretty sure he wouldn't be hearing from her.

Chapter TEN

Quinn always moved slowly, partly because it was her nature to take things easy and partly because she was six feet tall and not yet accustomed to a body that seemed to have outgrown her. When she tried to hurry she became clumsy and indecisive. Now, getting ready for her visit to Kay, she applied her makeup very carefully and then washed it all off again because it might give the wrong impression.

None of her clothes seemed sober enough for the occasion so she borrowed a black turtleneck sweater from Ben's closet. It was the proper color but too tight a fit and she was forced to cover it with the tan all-weather poncho she wore when she drove her little MG convertible at night or on windy days. Then she put on the only black skirt in her wardrobe, an ankle-length party skirt, and studied herself in the mirror.

Two things spoiled the effect she was attempting to create. The shoes she wore were her usual high-heeled sandals, and her long red hair hung loose over her shoulders, making her look what Ben would call too available. Unable to find a ribbon to tie her hair back, she borrowed a shoelace from one of Ben's oxfords. He'd be burned up when he discovered the sweater and the shoelace missing, but the confrontation would be brief. She would simply remove the shoelace and the sweater, and for good measure the skirt, and after that everything would be fine.

No, not this time.

"Not this time." She repeated the words aloud into the mirror. "The little beast will have to come crawling to me first and then maybe I'll consider it."

She fingered the swelling on her left cheekbone, already beginning to turn blue. It was the first time Ben had hit her and she'd been too surprised to strike back. She could easily have done so. She was taller than he was and nearly as heavy and she'd had a good deal of fighting experience with her two older brothers. Instead of striking back she burst into tears and that proved to be the best defense of all. Ben ran out the front door as if he were escaping a live volcano.

"He'll go to a bar down the street, have a couple of martinis and then come crawling back here, full of sorries. Well, I won't be here and I don't like sorries."

After a final look in the full-length mirror she went into the living room. Here the stereo was still going full blast the way Ben had turned it so the neighbors wouldn't hear any sounds of quarreling. She switched it off but the change in noise level was hardly noticeable. Traffic was heavy along the beachfront boulevard, the foghorns had begun to blow from the end of the breakwater and one of the oil platforms, gulls squawked and squabbled among themselves in the wake of fishing boats coming into the harbor with the day's catch.

She opened the front door at the same moment as Ben was about to enter. He held the key in his hand, pointed at her like a miniature knife. The martinis showed in his eyes and in his voice:

"Well, well. Going somewhere? No, don't tell me, let me guess. A Hallowe'en party and you're dressed up as Miss Salvation Army Thrift Shop."

"Let me past."

"Not yet." He pushed her back into the room and shut the door. "Where's the party?"

"I don't think you'd like to know."

"I think I would."

"Has anyone ever told you you can't hold your liquor?"

"Never. A recent Gallup poll indicated that ninety-nine and nine-tenths percent of the people never heard of me and wouldn't give a damn anyway. So where's the party?"

"There is no—"

"You can't attend a party without an escort. I hereby offer my services."

"Where I'm going you wouldn't be welcome."

"Home to mother?"

"Not *my* mother."

"You're too big to play cute. Whose mother?"

"Figure it out."

He tried to put his hands on her shoulders as if he intended to shake the truth out of her but she sidestepped beyond his reach. "I don't like what I'm figuring."

"Then it's probably correct."

"Kay," he said. "You're going to see Kay."

She half expected him to strike her and this time she was ready to defend herself. But instead he walked over to the window. Its only view was the side wall of Longo's Fish and Chip café next door. A delinquent with a can of spray paint had made an addition, FISH AND BULL CHIPS.

He said, "That's it, right? You're going to see Kay."

"Yes."

"I'm asking you not to do it."

"Really?"

"All right, I'm *begging* you not to do it."

"That's a little better but not good enough. Try bribery."

"Bribery?"

"You know. Money."

The gas heater in the room hadn't been turned on yet, and even under the wool turtleneck and the poncho and long skirt Quinn was shivering with cold. But Ben's face was sunburn-pink and sweat glistened across his forehead. She felt suddenly quite sorry for him and would have melted in his arms if he'd said the right thing. He didn't. Anyway, business was business.

He said, "How much do you want?"

"Half."

"Half of what?"

"If we were married I'd get half of everything under community-property laws, wouldn't I? And we're as good as married already, aren't we?" She knew she was on the wrong track but she couldn't seem to get off it or to brake herself to a stop. "I *feel* like your wife, Ben. I feel like we've been married three and a half months and this is our very first quarrel. And everything will turn out all right because we love each other. . . . Don't we?"

He stared at her without speaking.

"Me feeling married to you already, maybe that sounds silly to you."

"No."

"You don't think it's silly?"

"No. I think it's incredibly preposterously stupid and exactly what I'd expect from you."

"Don't you dare talk to me like—"

"Married. Jeez, what a laugh. You're a slut, a tramp who walked in off the street."

"That's a lie. You gave me a ride home from the Cielo theater when my car wouldn't start."

"Everything else started. You moved in the same night."

"It was at least a week later."

"Anyway, you turned out to be a pretty fair screw. Not great, but pretty fair."

"How would you know, you goddam pervert?"

He came toward her with his fists clenched but she ran out the door and down the narrow alley between the apartment building and Longo's Fish and Chip café.

Her little convertible was parked in one of the slots reserved for the café patrons. Mr. Longo himself hurried out the rear door as she was getting into the car.

He was angry. "I want you should stop parking in my customer slots."

"I've only been there fifteen minues."

"Two hours. I timed you. And never once you bought any fish and chips either."

"Lay off, will you? I got problems."

"I got customers." Mr. Longo wiped his forehead and neck with his greasy apron. "You young chicks think all you got to do is shake your boobs at any man and right away he gives you what you want. Lemme tell you, I seen plenty of boobs in my life and ain't one of them ever made me compromise my principles, which is business before pleasure."

"Listen, my boyfriend's after me to beat me up. Please let me out of here, will you? Please?"

"You gonna come in once in a while, buy some chips?"

"Sure, sure. Every day." He stepped back and she put the key in the ignition and revved the motor up. *Now go fry your balls, you old goat.*

Quinn had seen the house only once before, several nights previously. It was late and she and Ben had been drinking. The very size of the house had intimidated her and she wanted to turn around and go home. But Ben kept saying, "Come on, baby," in the half coaxing, half bullying tone she usually responded to.

"I'm scared, Benjie. What if the dogs—"

"They won't bother us. They sleep in the kitchen at the rear of the house."

"My feet hurt."

"Take your shoes off."

"We should have brought the Porsche up."

"Too noisy."

So the Porsche remained on the street below.

Ben carried her shoes for her while she walked barefoot on the grass alongside the driveway. The grass was cold and wet and almost immediately she began to shiver.

Ben was very considerate. "Here, take my coat."

"Then you'll be cold."

"No. I'm burning up."

She knew from the way he put his coat around her shoulders that he was going to make love to her in the child's playhouse that he called the palace.

She turned her head so her cheek brushed the back of his hand. "The bed will be too small, won't it?"

"If we can make it in the Porsche we can make it anywhere."

She giggled and hung on to his arm and everything seemed fun as it always did when Ben was in a good mood.

It didn't last. Even before they reached the palace she sensed that his excitement was different this time, hardly connected with her at all.

There was a full moon and she could see the palace door quite clearly, carved with brightly painted figures, a little girl sitting on a throne with her hand on the head of a black dog, a king and queen dancing, a court jester, a tree with golden apples.

"Someone went to a lot of trouble for an ordinary playhouse."

"Not someone. Me. And it's not an ordinary playhouse. It's the palace of a princess."

"Did you do all that carving?"

"Yes."

"Why?"

"I told you."

Ben opened the door and switched on an overhead light and a lamp. "Come in."

"I don't want to."

"You said you did."

"I was sort of drunk."

"This is a hell of a time to sober up."

"I wasn't as drunk as you to begin with."

"Jesus Christ, are we going to stand here arguing about

which one of us was drunker?" He pulled her into the room and kicked the door shut.

Everything in the palace was built to scale, not for a child as young as Annamay, but for a rather small adult. Quinn could stand up straight but her head grazed the ceiling and she stooped instinctively the way she used to when she first started to grow faster than her peers.

"Why did you make the ceiling so low?"

"To remind adults that this is not their place, it belongs to the princess and her duke."

"You're kind of crazy, aren't you?"

"Not kind of. Very."

"I don't believe it. I read in a magazine once that people who are really crazy don't know it."

"I'm an exception."

"Stop talking like that. You're making me nervous."

"All grown-ups are supposed to feel nervous in the palace. It's not their place."

"Then why are we here?"

"I belong," he said. "I belong."

The tone of his voice, the musty smell in the room, the threatening touch of the ceiling against her head increased her anxiety. Trying not to show it she sat down on the small bird-and-flower·print davenport. Ben stood looking down at her frowning, her sandals still in his hand.

"God, you have big feet."

"What of it?"

"They're as big as mine."

"No, they're not."

"Want to bet?"

He sat down beside her on the davenport, slipped off the leather moccasins he was wearing and put on the high-heeled sandals. His hands shook as he buckled the straps and stood up.

"See? They fit exactly. You lose."

"I didn't bet. Now give me back my shoes."

He pretended not to hear her. He was walking around the room, not awkwardly the way men in drag did on television or in the movies, but quite gracefully and naturally as if he'd been doing it all his life.

She watched him, first in disbelief, then in anger. "What are you, some kind of freako? Give me back my shoes. I want to go home."

"Why? The fun's only beginning."

"I don't think this is fun, watching some guy prance around in women's shoes."

"It's a game."

"I don't care. I hate it."

"Come on, baby, dance with me."

"Leave me alone."

"Okay, I'll dance with the kiddies." He picked up the two dolls from the bunk bed, Marietta with her half-bald head and Luella Lu with her glued-in eye. Holding them close against his chest he began circling the room. "They're Annamay's children so of course they love dancing as she did. The princess and I often danced. Round and round, just like this. Round and round—"

When he passed the davenport she reached out with one foot and caught him on the shin. He stumbled and fell to the floor, the dolls flying out of his arms like caged birds unexpectedly released. He winced as he picked himself up, holding his left elbow with his right hand.

"You tripped me, you bitch."

"Open the door and let me out of here or I'll scream."

"Chances are you're a good screamer. Right?"

"The best."

"Give us a sample."

"If I scream your fancy friends will come running and want to know why you busted into their kid's playhouse."

"It's not a playhouse. It's real, it's a real palace."

"This kinky stuff makes me sick. Let me out before I throw up all over the royal rug."

He looked at her soberly, bitterly. "You're not fit to be in this place anyway."

"Good. Then I'll leave."

"Beat it, you tramp."

He stepped away from the door and she darted outside without waiting for her shoes. She started down the driveway, running barefooted in the wet grass.

By the time she reached the Porsche parked on the street she was out of breath but quite calm. Ben had left the car unlocked so she opened the door and dropped into the single passenger seat and waited.

She didn't have long to wait. About five minutes later Ben appeared and got into the car without saying anything or even looking at her. He was wearing his own leather moccasins.

She said, "Where are my shoes?"

"I put them someplace. I don't remember."

"But I want—"

"Forget it. I'll pay you for them. How much?"

"They cost me a fortune."

"You probably bought them at a garage sale. I'll give you ten bucks."

"Fifty."

"Twenty-five."

"What a cheapskate you are. You live in a dump, you never take me anyplace, you drive this broken-down hunk of tin that sounds like a truck."

"Broken-down hunk of tin?" He sounded outraged. "Jeez, you're ignorant. This is a classic three fifty-six Speedster."

"Big deal."

"If you don't like it, get out and walk. Feel like walking?"

"No." She leaned her head against the back of the seat and closed her eyes. "I'm tired, Benjie. Take me home."

"Where's home?"

"The apartment."

"Why would you want to go back to a cheap little dump like that?"

"Because it's our place, Benjie, yours and mine. And I don't mind it being a dump, really. I mean, I never had things so great at home either."

He released the hand brake and let the car roll halfway down the hill before starting the engine. It was hard to talk above the noise and neither of them tried. But when they pulled into the parking lot behind the apartment building Ben said quietly, "I'm sorry. I got drunk and did a lot of crazy things and I'm sorry."

"It wasn't the real you, Benjie."

"What if it was?"

"I wouldn't care. I mean, I'd care, sure, but I'd still want to marry you."

"*Marry* me?"

"Why not? I think that deep down inside what you really want is a child of your own. I can give you one. And maybe she'll grow up to be like Annamay and you can build her a playhouse. And if you want to call it a palace, that's okay with me."

"Out," he said. "Get out of the car."

"Why? I thought we'd sit here and have a nice little talk."

"This nice little talk is heap big crap."

"I only wanted to cheer you up."

"I am not cheered by references to marriage and related subjects. You know nothing, understand nothing. So shut up. I'll pay you fifty bucks for the shoes."

"I won't take it."

"Why not? It's what you asked for to begin with."

"I didn't pick them up at a garage sale like you said but I bought them at that discount store on lower State Street for fourteen ninety-five."

"All right, I'll pay you fourteen ninety-five."

"Plus tax."

"Plus tax."

"I never cheated anyone in my life. Since you lost my shoes it's only fair you should pay for them but no more than I did."

"Will you shut up about those goddam shoes?"

"Sure I will," she said. *For now.*

The *now* didn't last long.

Three days later she found herself at the Hyatts' front door.

Kay opened the door herself. It was the first time Quinn had seen her except for a news photo taken as she came out of the coroner's inquest. Quinn had found the picture among a sheaf of newspaper clippings in the bottom drawer of Ben's bureau. It showed a woman with her head partly turned away from the camera, one hand shielding her eyes from flashbulbs. That there were other pictures of Kay in Ben's possession Quinn was certain but she had never been able to locate them, and when she asked questions his answers were either evasive or deliberately provocative: Kay was beautiful, stunning, mysterious, anything he could think of to make her jealous.

Kay Hyatt didn't fit any of those descriptions. She was a small slim woman with rather drab blond hair and a tan that was beginning to fade with the approach of winter. She wore a plain brown wool suit and no jewelry except a gold wedding band. Her green eyes looked at Quinn with a penetrating directness as if they were seeing things that weren't supposed to be visible. She didn't speak.

After a time Quinn said in a thin tight voice that was too small for her:

"I'm Quinn."

"Yes."

"We talked on the phone."

"Yes."

Quinn gave a nervous little laugh. "You must think I'm pretty brassy to come charging over like this."

"I haven't known you long enough to form an opinion."

"Doesn't Ben tell you about me?"

"No."

"Not anything? Ever?"

"No. Come inside," Kay said. "It's too cold to talk out here."

Quinn went in, keeping her hands hidden under the poncho so Kay wouldn't see she was trembling with anxiety and indecision.

Once the door closed behind her, all outside noises were shut out and inside noises were absorbed by the spongy material that covered the floor and walls. To Quinn, accustomed to the continual sounds of the harbor and beachfront traffic, the silence was disturbing. She wanted to hear footsteps, voices, the sounds of life. But there was only this empty air, like a hole waiting to be filled. Quinn tried to fill it by talking loudly and rapidly as she followed Kay across the hall to the living room.

"He should have told you about me. We've been living together for three and a half months and we're going to be married. At least we *were* going to be married until lately when he began taking you to concerts and stuff. Want to hear the truth? Ben don't—doesn't know beans about music. He told me one night when he was drunk. He just sits there pretending to listen while he thinks about other things like what he's going to have for dinner. All he really knows is how to pronounce composers' names right, like Wagner for example. Vog-ner treated his varicose veins with vodka."

"Indeed? Was the treatment successful?"

"No no, it's not really true, it's how I'm supposed to remember about *v*'s and *w*'s. Which I do, but it doesn't make sense to me. A *v* is a *v* and a *w* is a *w*."

"I hope you don't have to go through the whole alphabet to come to the point."

"I already came to it. Ben and I would be married next month or week, maybe even tomorrow, if you weren't in the picture."

"Is that your idea or his?"

"Every man needs a nudge to get married. So I nudge."

"I was referring," Kay said, "to the part about me. How do I fit into what you call the picture?"

Quinn hesitated for a moment, squinting in concentration. "Ben has this thing about you. It's not ordinary love, I could handle that easy. But this other, it's queer, and in some way Annamay is—was a part of it."

"Ben is a friend of the family."

"That's not enough for him. He wants to be *in* the family, to be a member of it, to live in this house and play in the palace like Annamay. It's funny how grown-up he is in some ways, if you know what I mean. But in other ways he's a little boy, pretending crazy stuff like he's of royal blood because his last name happens to be York. After he's had a few drinks and we're in bed, he tells me a lot of things like that, especially if he thinks I'm sleeping, or just as drunk as he is."

"I have never seen Ben drunk."

"Around you he'd be careful," Quinn said. "Around me he figures, what's he got to lose?"

"Does he often drink too much?"

"No oftener than a dozen other guys I've—I know. Usually he's fun after a few drinks and he pulls silly stunts like the other night when he brought me to the palace. It started out to be fun, anyway."

"He brought you here, to Annamay's palace?"

"Yes."

"Why?"

"Well, like I said, it started out as fun, a fun thing to do. Then it kind of got out of hand. He went a little crazy. He

174

put on my sandals and began dancing around the room with the two dolls in his arms, getting more and more excited. It scared me. I mean, I hardly knew who he was, what he was."

"Is this what you came here to tell me?"

"Some of it. There's more."

"I've heard enough."

"Plenty more. Oh, he puts on a great front for you, pretending to be so highbrow and classy. He's no classier than I am. Which is maybe why I understand him. I don't expect a guy to act one hundred percent normal all the time. Let Ben have his freaky times."

"I want you to leave, Miss Quinn."

"But—"

"Now."

"Okay," Quinn said. "Sure."

The two women walked in silence out into the hall to the front door. When the door opened the cold moist air of late afternoon drifted in, carrying the sounds of a live world into the dead hall.

Quinn took a long deep breath. "I only told you what you ought to know."

"That a family friend had unnatural feelings about me and my daughter?"

"All I meant was, he has freaky times."

"And in one of those freaky times he might have done something improper, may even have killed her. Is this what you're suggesting?"

"No, no. I didn't—I never said—my God, he adored her. All his violence was directed against *me*. This bruise on my cheek, that was when he tried to stop me from coming here today. But I don't stop easy, not when the stakes are high. I want to marry Ben. I want to live in a house like this some day, only noisier, you know, kids and stuff. Ben needs a family of his own, maybe a little girl like Annamay, I can give it to him."

"Get out of here, you insensitive clod."

"I don't care what you call me," Quinn said. But she was talking to a closed door.

She had left the top down on her convertible and the seat and back and dashboard were as wet as if someone had turned a hose on them. There was a blanket in the trunk which she could have used to wipe off the seat but she didn't bother. She sat in the little puddles of water, feeling the moisture seep through her skirt and into her bones. By the time she reached the apartment house the chill had spread up her spine and into her head.

The parking lot was full as usual, so she parked her car in one of the slots reserved for the customers of Longo's Fish and Chips. Then, shivering, teeth chattering, she went into the café by the rear door, sat at the counter and ordered a cup of coffee and a bag of chips.

She drank the coffee while she was waiting for the chips to cook.

Mr. Longo watched her through his thick glasses.

"This don't entitle you to park all night," he said. "One hour's the limit. One. Like in numero uno. Savvy?"

"I can hear."

"Your boyfriend drive a white Porsche?"

"Yes."

"He took off right after you did. I guess he didn't catch up with you. You don't look beat up to me."

"Don't I?"

"Unless you got bruises where they don't show."

"If I have, you're not going to see them. Savvy?"

She ate the chips with a sprinkle of vinegar and a dash of salt. Mr. Longo kept watching her as though he'd never seen anybody eat before.

"So you got bruises where they don't show, huh?"

"What's it to you?"

"It kind of interests me. I wonder where they are."

176

"Keep wondering."

"Oh, I will. Count on it."

"You owe me a month's free parking just for the way you're looking at me, you old goat."

"Shit. Pretty girls are a dime a dozen."

"Okay, here's a dime. Get yourself a dozen and leave me alone."

The chips tasted rancid, the counter bore water stains and cigarette burns, Mr. Longo's apron was dirty. She half closed her eyes and tried to picture her future with Ben, the church wedding, the big house with the happy noisy children. But she couldn't see past Mr. Longo's dirty apron and grease-spotted glasses.

She left the café without paying. Mr. Longo didn't say a word.

When she returned to the apartment she found a man who was a stranger to her standing in the hall outside the door marked QUINN, YORK. He was a tall thin man with graying hair and a shabby brown suit. His face looked rather shabby too, as if he'd worn it too many times without pressing.

Quinn said, "That's my place."

"You're Miss Quinn?"

"Yes."

"I'm Michael Dunlop, a friend of Mr. York. Mrs. Hyatt called me and asked me to come over and talk to him."

"He's not here."

"Perhaps I could wait for him."

"It won't do much good," she said, but she unlocked the door and went inside and switched on a couple of table lamps. She didn't ask him in so he stood in the doorway.

"When do you expect him, Miss Quinn?"

"I don't."

"Even if you had an argument he has to come home sometime."

"Home? You call this dump a home?"

"He lives here, doesn't he?"

"That's not the same thing." She turned on the wall gas heater and stood in front of it, massaging her hands to warm them. "He doesn't *live* here. He parks his butt here like he parks his Porsche. Home." She repeated the word as though it had the rancid taste of Mr. Longo's chips. "Home is the kind of place Mrs. Hyatt lives in. He'd like to live there too but he never will. I fixed it so he never will."

"How did you do that, Miss Quinn?"

"I told her a few things about him. A very few, considering what I *could* have told her."

"It's chilly out here in the hall," Michael said. "Do you mind if I come inside?"

"Why bother? It won't do any good to wait for him. He's not coming back, not tonight anyway. He'll find some bar, have a few drinks, then go for a long fast ride maybe with some chick he's latched on to. If he gets picked up by the cops on a five-oh-two and needs someone to bail him out, he won't call you or the Hyatts or any of their crowd. He'll call *me* because I'm his real friend, I'll come up with the money, no questions asked."

"You sound as though that's what you're expecting to happen."

"It wouldn't be the first time."

Michael went in and closed the door after him. "So you consider yourself his best friend, Miss Quinn."

"We're also lovers."

"Some of the things you implied about him to Mrs. Hyatt were neither friendly nor loving."

"I was mad."

"So you were speaking as a jealous woman rather than as a concerned citizen willing to go to the police and repeat the allegations."

"The police? Are you crazy? Why would I want to mess with them?"

"In the interests of justice."

178

"Justice? Why, they couldn't even find my car when it was stolen. And when it turned up in Bakersfield and my mother had to drive me over to pick it up, they wouldn't even pay for the gas. Some justice. And it had two flat tires."

"I don't think you're aware of the seriousness of some of your allegations concerning Mr. York."

She stared at him in silence for some time, her full mouth getting thinner and thinner until it became a straight ugly line. "You can't make me go to the police. And if you send them here I'll clam up, I won't say a word. I won't even be here. I'm getting out." A tear trickled down her left cheek and she slapped it away with the palm of her hand as if it were a fly. "Let him wait for me for a change. Let him wonder what bar I'm in and who I'm picking up."

"Miss Quinn—"

"Let him think the same rotten thoughts I've had to think."

"Miss Quinn, more is involved here than a quarrel between you and Mr. York. If you know of any suspicious incident involving him and the Hyatt girl, you owe it to her parents to speak up."

"I owe nobody nothing," she said and slapped at another tear. "Now leave me alone. I got to think. I got to *think*."

"I wish I could help you."

"You can help me. Bug off."

"All right."

He went out into the hall. Through the closed door he could hear her sobbing and slamming things around. She was a noisy thinker.

Driving home he listened to the six o'clock news. The outside world hadn't changed much in the past twenty-four hours. The situation in Poland was worsening. Labor unrest in Western Europe was increasing. An earthquake had shaken Chile and a typhoon had hit the Philippines. The county Board of Supervisors was split on a growth, no-growth decision. An attempted downtown bank robbery had been thwarted. There was a twenty percent chance of rain in the mountain areas and a local woman had received a telegram from the President congratulating her on her hundredth birthday. A white sports car driven at a high rate of speed had gone over the cliff into the ocean on Miramar Road. The occupant or occupants were presumed dead. Rescue work could not begin until daylight.

Chapter ELEVEN

There was no funeral. The coffin was a plastic box with a handle like a suitcase, and the taped organ music could hardly be heard above the laboring engine of the burial boat, *Valhalla,* as it fought a heavy sea to get beyond the two-mile limit. Coast Guard regulations for a boat that size permitted no more than five mourners, and of these, two were seasick before the boat left the dock. The captain of the *Valhalla* had wanted to postpone the trip until a calmer day but Howard, the executor of Ben's estate, insisted that the ashes be disposed of as soon as possible.

And so Chizzy hung over the rail with a handkerchief provided by Michael held to her mouth. Standing beside her, Quinn alternately sobbed and threw up. She had come on board carrying a single white rose but it had disappeared during her first upheaval, and so there were no flowers.

There was no eulogy. Kay put her hand on the plastic box and said, "Good-bye, Ben." The box was dropped overboard and almost immediately disappeared among the whitecaps.

A crewman provided towels for the two seasick women and told them to breathe deeply and pinch their left earlobes.

"That's silly," Chizzy said, but she obeyed instructions because she would have done anything, within reason or without, to improve her condition.

Quinn kept gasping and sobbing about the white rose she had bought for Ben at a real florist's and lost overboard.

"A rose won't do him any good if he's guilty," the crewman said. "And if he's got a clean slate he won't need flowers."

"Guilty? Guilty of what?"

"There's talk."

There was talk. From the sagging frame dwellings of the barrio to the mansions on the bluffs overlooking the sea.

When Howard went to work in the mornings a sudden hush fell over the office as if he had interrupted a secret session, a kangaroo court. When Kay's friends called they said the right things but some of their voices carried half-tones of suppressed excitement, and others sounded tight as though questions were being swallowed.

There was talk.

Ernestina, the maid next door to the Hyatts, heard about it at La Casa de la Raza and came over to ask Chizzy for the real truth.

Chizzy was severe with her. "You mustn't listen to gossip."

"I no listen. My ears, they listen."

"Okay, I'm talking to your ears, so pay attention. Benjamin York was a fine young man, pure as the driven snow."

"Snow, huh? White stuff?"

"Don't play dumb with me. You know what snow is. You Mexicans waste a lot of time pretending you don't understand."

"I understand good," Ernestina said, and proved it that night at the Casa by informing her friends that Ben was a cocaine addict who could afford to buy the pure stuff which had then driven him to crime.

Dru heard the talk at school and at home.

At school the talk was direct. She was sought out in the

halls before classes began and in the cloakrooms at recess where the older girls gathered to smoke and discuss sex and its deviations.

"Did you really *know* him?"

"I saw him all the time."

"Oh, my God, maybe you were almost murdered."

"Maybe," Dru said. "Almost."

"Just imagine, almost being murdered."

Everyone imagined, shuddered, puffed and blew the smoke out the windows with a hair dryer.

"Were you ever *alone* with him?"

"Sure."

"Did he ask you to take your clothes off?"

"I think he sort of hinted."

"Did he ever touch you in any of those places you're not supposed to let anyone touch?"

Dru, torn between the truth and her new celebrity status as the girl who was almost murdered, chose to compromise:

"I didn't let him."

"Couldn't you *tell* he was a sex maniac?"

"My parents never allow me to go to movies about sex maniacs so I don't know what one looks like."

In the discussion that followed it was agreed that parents were grossly unfair and stupid not to permit young people to attend whatever movies they wanted to in the interests of furthering their education.

The talk Dru heard at home was indirect. Ben's name was not mentioned in her presence, but she was well aware they talked about him after she went to bed. And so, when reminded of bedtime, she dutifully went up to her room, put on her nightclothes and turned up the volume of her television set. Then she crept back downstairs in the dark.

Vicki and John were in the den where they often went to hold conversations they meant to be kept private behind the heavy oak door. But tonight the fire John had set in the fireplace burned too fast and overheated the small room so the door had to be opened. It was a stroke of luck for Dru. Barely halfway down the steps she could hear their voices quite clearly, mostly Vicki's with its high-pitched twittering persistence:

"—from Darien Angelo whose first cousin works in the D.A.'s office so it must be true."

"Why? What does she do in the D.A.'s office, read minds?"

"She pays attention. She listens."

"And tells."

"She doesn't tell just everybody, only her relatives."

"And *they* tell everybody."

"Stop being so negative and you might learn something," Vicki said. "Officially, the case of Annamay's death is still open. But unofficially there isn't a person in the department who's not convinced that Ben killed himself out of remorse for his crime."

"Which one, speeding or drunk driving? That's all that can be proved against him."

"Are you going to keep on like this, taking his side?"

"I'm trying to be fair."

"Fair? What's fair anymore in this world? The word doesn't have any meaning."

"Not with Darien Angelo's first cousin in the D.A.'s office."

"Very well, if you won't listen, I won't talk," Vicki said, and for nearly half a minute she didn't. Then, "I spent the afternoon over at Kay's house. She and Howard refuse to discuss Ben's death, even with me, Kay's own sister. But I can't help feeling it's the best thing that could have happened as far as their marriage is concerned."

"That's your opinion, is it, that Ben did everyone a favor by driving over a cliff?"

"Not everyone, of course. I'm sure that Quinn woman is suffering to a certain extent. But on the whole, I think it's all for the best."

"You," John said, "are a very crude little lady."

"And you science freaks are so skeptical you won't face facts until all the *i*'s are dotted and the *t*'s crossed."

"Toss me a fact."

"I already did. Ben's death is drawing Kay and Howard closer together. I could see it happening right in front of my eyes."

"Are you sure you haven't got your *t*'s dotted and your eyes crossed?"

"Make all the sardonic remarks you like. Kay and Howard are acting like—well, like married people again. They seem to be back where they started. Maybe they'll even adopt a child, though frankly I can't see why people are so hyped on having kids. I mean, look what can happen."

And Dru, crouched on the steps listening, thought, *She means me. I'm what happened.*

She went upstairs to her room, turned off the television set and climbed into bed. There was a cold hard lump in her throat like an ice cube that couldn't be swallowed, couldn't be coughed up, wouldn't melt. *Look what can happen. She means me.*

Dru pulled the covers up over her head, over her ugly face, her stringy brown hair, her beady little eyes, her nose that was too big and her chin that was too small.

She means me. I happened.

Chapter TWELVE

Madam Firenze was in a foul mood. Unable to locate her hoard of raisins, she accused Ms. Leigh of stealing them for her own use.

"What raisins, madam?"

"You know what raisins. The ones I pick out of my cereal in the mornings to save for the champagne in case it goes flat. You took them."

"I don't drink champagne," Ms. Leigh said imperturbably. "Neither, as a matter of fact, do you."

"I would if they let me."

"Face it, madam. They're not going to let you. You're hard enough to deal with when you're sober."

"They might give me some for my birthday."

"If they do, it'll be the two-buck-a-bottle kind you can pick up in a grocery store, not worth wasting your raisins on. Besides, your birthday was last month. You have eleven whole months to start a new collection."

"I want my old collection." Madam's watery voice was heating up like a steam whistle and getting ready to blow. "Give them back right this minute."

"I don't have them. I have no reason to have raisins."

"You give them back or get out of this house. Forever."

"Forever is a long time."

"Not long enough, you thief. Leave this house immediately. You hear me?"

"Madam, everyone this side of the Colorado River can hear you."

"Get, get, get!"

Ms. Leigh got.

From a phone booth at the nearest gas station she called one of the two numbers Michael Dunlop had given her. There was no answer so she called the second.

A man's voice said, "Hello."

"Mr. Dunlop?"

"Yes."

"This is Tai Leigh, Madam Firenze's companion, for want of a better word. I have the material you asked me to gather for you. Do you still want it?"

He had forgotten about it but he managed to say with conviction, "Of course I do. Shall I come over and pick it up?"

"No, no. Firenze just ordered me off the premises forever, which means I have a couple of free hours before she starts yelling for me again. I can bring the stuff over to you now."

"Fine."

"Do you live in that house connected with the church? What's a place like that called, by the way?"

"When the roof doesn't leak and the plumbing works, I call it a house. I have other names for other occasions."

"Have people ever told you you talk funny for a minister?"

"People have and I do," Michael said. "When can I expect you?"

"Fifteen minutes."

She arrived within a minute of the specified time, looking cool and elegant in a green suede coat with matching boots. As soon as she stepped into the hall she made the place appear smaller and shabbier, and Michael somehow felt the need to apologize.

"Excuse the way things look," he said. "I've been baching it for a while. My wife's away."

"Home to mother?"

"Aunt."

"I'm sorry, I thought I was being funny."

"And you were," Michael said. "There's certainly an element of humor in having one's future decided by a spinster aunt with a low opinion of men."

"Gosh, I really goofed, didn't I?"

"Forget it. Come in the living room and show me the material."

"I'm afraid it's too little and too late."

"Too little, maybe. Too late, why?"

She seemed surprised by the question. "I thought Mr. York's death made it obvious that he—"

"There is a presumption of innocence in this country's legal system. Mr. York's death makes it impossible to prove he is guilty so he must be considered innocent. Isn't that reasonable?"

"Sure. But it doesn't stop the talk going round. People don't want to be reasonable. It's dull. Believing Mr. York is a murderer perks up the drab little image they see in their mirror. That's the way it works. Sorry."

"So am I."

Ms. Leigh unzipped the leather case she was carrying and removed some sheets of paper containing lines of typing with handwritten notes in the margins.

"I repeat, there's very little here, considering the amount of trash I had to wade through, gibberish, profanity, clichés, old burlesque jokes, you name it. But here are the parts I thought were pertinent. Can you read my handwriting in the margins?"

In contrast to her appearance and manner, Ms. Leigh's handwriting was wildly unpredictable. Words ran together or were separated in the middle. No letters were capitalized and punctuation was mainly confined to question and exclamation marks.

"I think I can make it out," Michael said.

"Maybe I'd better stay and go over it with you."

"Thanks. I'd appreciate that."

"None of it's dated. I told you, I'm not a secretary, I'm a writer. But I may be able to throw some light on a few things. For instance, here's a paragraph in which she describes being chased and attacked by a pack of wild animals. 'Wolves and bears snapping at my legs, their teeth red with my blood.' The basis for that fantasy is fairly obvious. The Hyatts have a German shepherd which resembles a wolf and a very large black dog which could be mistaken for a bear by someone in Firenze's condition. Nearly all her fearful imaginings have some reality behind them. Here's another section where she describes being pelted by huge rocks. And sure enough, she did come home one day with a swelling and some scratches on her forehead. She was so convincing, so positive that someone had thrown rocks at her that I decided I'd better investigate. I ruined a pair of shoes walking half a mile or so up the creek and came across an area where a couple of bunya bunya trees had been planted. Are you familiar with them?"

"I don't think so."

"They bear pods as big as a man's head and correspondingly heavy. Being hit by one is so serious that in county and city parks when these trees are shedding, their perimeters are roped off and warning signs posted. So I think we can safely assume that no one had pelted her with rocks. She was simply under the wrong tree at the wrong time. You agree?"

"Yes."

"The origins of some of her other fears and fancies are more obscure. At one point she claims she was attacked by bats who flew into her face and got entangled in her hair. I tried to explain to her that bats are nocturnal animals and she wouldn't be likely to run into any in the afternoon. If I had to guess at what she thought were bats I'd say sycamore leaves. They're so large that one of them blowing into a person's face could scare the daylights out of her providing there weren't too many daylights to begin with.... Is she coming back?"

"Who?"

"Your wife."

"I don't know," Michael said. "Even if she does, there'll be so many strings attached, so many conditions, provisos, whereases, that I won't be able to live up to them anyway."

"Will you try?"

"Probably not." He paused. "Lorna was a minister's daughter and she likes being a minister's wife, the attention, the prestige of a sort, the various roles she's expected to play."

"Then what would keep her away?"

"I submitted my resignation several days ago."

"And that's that?"

"That's that. Over and out. Let's get back to Firenze."

"All right." Ms. Leigh turned to another of the typewritten pages. "She complains a number of times about being shot at by a sniper trying to prevent her from finishing her memoirs. The bullets were probably eucalyptus pods or acorns from the live oak trees. But the last two references here baffle me. I'm pretty sure they refer to the day the Hyatt child disappeared because Firenze talks about the devil wind and that was the day we had our first santa ana of the season. It came up very suddenly and caught her as she was wandering along the creek. She was terrified. She came home screaming about a ghost that floated through the air, changing shape like ectoplasm. She didn't know whether it was a man or a woman, only that it was out to punish her."

"It was a man." Michael explained about Mr. Cassandra and his visits to the creek to refresh himself in the water and breathe the country air. The sight of him in his white robe at the height of a santa ana would be enough to frighten even a normal person.

"I'm glad to hear she wasn't just imagining the whole

thing," Ms. Leigh said. "Maybe she's not as kooky as I thought."

"Maybe not."

"I'm afraid all this isn't being much help to you. Shall I go on anyway?"

"Please do."

Ms. Leigh had reached the last page of the typescript. She glanced over it, frowning. "The wind was the main theme. She talked of banshee noises, leaves rustling like hellfire, bullets striking her head, children screaming, children blowing out of trees, floating through the air like kites. Children play a big role in all her nightmares so I more or less discounted that part. As for the kite, she may actually have seen one but it's most unlikely in a wind like that. Later, when I was transcribing, I asked her about it. She denied mentioning kites or children or hellfire or banshee noises or any of the rest of it. She claimed the voice on the tape was that of an impersonator. And she called me, among other things, a cheat, a liar, a flat-chested chink, a spy for the IRS and a lousy typist. . . . Ah well, nobody's perfect."

Ms. Leigh put the papers back in the leather folder.

"So there you have it. Not much, but the best I could do."

"You were promised a fee for your services."

"Forget it. The whole thing's been a lesson to me and I'm always willing to pay for lessons."

"What did you learn?"

"As I told you the day we met, I planned on writing a book about her writing a book. Now I realize, after going through all this crap, that I simply don't have the perseverance or patience. I'd end up in a rubber room accusing myself of being an imposter."

"I'm glad you've been spared that fate."

"So am I. In fact, I'm quitting the job. Larry and I are moving to L.A. to be closer to the action. I think Larry has a great future in television commercials."

"Good luck to both of you."

"Thanks. What about you?"

"I don't see much future for myself in television commercials," Michael said. "But I expect to survive."

They shook hands and Ms. Leigh stepped briskly out into the morning sun. The wind didn't bend a line of her geometric hairdo. It reflected the sun's rays like black glass.

Michael watched as she backed into her miniature car, folded her long legs under the steering wheel, slammed the door shut and sped away from the curb as if she were determined to stay ahead of whatever was behind her. He wished he could go with her.

Chapter THIRTEEN

The old man sat in the redwood chair beside the koi pond, his face almost hidden by a battered straw hat. It was his favorite hat. He'd found it in the avocado grove where it had been dropped by one of the Mexican pickers, and it was so big it bent the tops of his ears over. But it had convenient holes in the crown which allowed air to circulate. And he had not, in spite of Chizzy's repeated warnings, contracted any scalp disorders from it, head lice or scabies or mites.

Under its wide brim he alternately dozed, listened to the gentle waterfall, watched the brilliant koi moving back and forth and round and round like a painting in progress.

Only the giant black magoi was not part of this moving picture. He lay motionless at the bottom of the pond. The gold piece on his forehead seemed to have tarnished and his diamond scales looked dusty. When the other fish came to the surface to feed on the pellets Mr. Hyatt threw in for them the magoi didn't stir.

He may be sick, the old man thought. Perhaps we should call the Japanese man who doctors koi, gives them antibiotics, even operates after slowing their metabolism with sedatives.

He knew the magoi couldn't hear him from way down at the bottom of the pond, and certainly was too stupid to understand him, but he couldn't stop himself from talking to him, calling him by name.

"Are you sick, Hikari? Do you want me to call the fish doctor? Or do you want to be left alone like me? I have only a few years left but you have possibly a hundred. Does that prospect depress you?"

He watched for signs the magoi had heard him. There were none. Fish remembered no past, anticipated no future. Yet in his native habitat the magoi struggled with great courage to survive, fighting his way up rivers and over waterfalls like a salmon. Here, in this quiet pond, there was nothing to fight, no rivers with rushing currents, no waterfalls except the small man-made one with nothing at the top but clumps of ferns hiding an electric pump. And even if he were taken to a stream and given his freedom he wouldn't know what to do with it. He would swim round and round as if he were still in the pond, and wait for someone to throw him pellets of food.

Like me, the old man thought. My boundaries are more extensive but they are just as inflexible as the concrete and tile ones of the pond. And I wait for Chizzy to throw me pellets of food and for Howard to tell me what to do, and for Kay to look after me when I'm sick. Kay is my fish doctor.

His shoulders and belly began to shake with silent laughter as he pictured the look on Kay's face if he told her she was his fish doctor. She would probably call Howard and Chizzy, perhaps Michael too, and the four of them would decide that he had finally gone over the hill.

He laughed until the tears came to his eyes, blurring his vision so he didn't see Michael approaching from the other side of the pond.

"Mr. Hyatt, may I bother you for a minute?"

"Why Michael, I was just—just sort of thinking of you."

"Have you seen Dru?"

"No. I wasn't expecting her. She doesn't come to visit me anymore. We had what you might call a misunderstanding."

"I went to her house to ask her some questions," Michael said. "She wasn't there. She didn't come home from school."

194

"It's still fairly early in the day." He took out his pocket watch. "Oh dear, it's not, is it? Now and then I lose track of time."

"She always takes the same bus home. She was on it when it left the school but she didn't get off. Or if she did, she vanished right afterward."

"Vanished, that's an ugly word. You mustn't use that word, Michael."

"I have to. Her parents are searching the neighborhood around her house, and Howard and Kay have gone to question the driver of the school bus and the children who were on it."

"Have they called the police?"

"They're waiting for some scrap of information. She's an independent child who often goes off on her own. I thought she might have come here and we'd find her in the palace."

Mr. Hyatt shook his head. "No. She doesn't come here anymore. We had words."

"What about?"

"I said something cruel to her, not meaning to be cruel, only to help her. She kept talking about Annamay not really being dead, how she had gotten up and walked away and the bones that were buried were animal bones. She was so convincing and I wanted so terribly to believe it that I became angry. I was too harsh with her. I called her a deluded little girl. And she—she called me a crazy old man. Tell me truthfully, Michael. Do you think I'm a crazy old man?"

"No."

"I'm forgetful. That worries me. Is it possible that I did something shameful and then completely forgot about it? Do you consider that possible?"

"No."

"But you're not sure."

"I'm sure."

"I'm not," Mr. Hyatt said slowly. "I'll never be sure. It is a terrifying thing to doubt one's own mind. But from now on I always will."

"Doubts are a part of living."

"Not ones like this. She accused me—"

"Don't dwell on it, Mr. Hyatt. It was the talk of a troubled child." He helped the old man to his feet. "Come on, we'd better search the palace."

"We won't find her."

"We have to try. I need you to open the door for me."

When they rounded the last bend in the path they could both see that the door was already open. Without a word the old man turned and began walking back toward the koi pond.

The first time Michael had seen the palace it had an abandoned look, with leaves and dust scattered over the floor and furniture, the cushions in disarray on the davenport, a teacup in the sink, the closet filled with toys and old clothes and the fateful pair of sandals. The sandals were gone now and so were the clothes. The closet contained only a neat row of Annamay's dolls and stuffed toys. The leaves and dirt had been swept away, the cushions rearranged on the davenport, the teacup washed and put in the cupboard. Instead of looking abandoned the room appeared ready to receive a new royal princess or perhaps a visitor like the short fat woman who sat at the dining table. She wore an apron and a tea towel wrapped around her head to protect her hair from dust. She stared at Michael, unsmiling.

"Miss Kay and I were cleaning," she said, as though an explanation had been demanded from her. "She took a box of clothes over to the house and I haven't seen her since. I went ahead with the cleaning, thinking she'd be coming back any minute."

"She and Howard went to search for Dru," Michael said. "Dru didn't arrive home from school. Has she been here?"

"Not for a long time. She doesn't stop in for cookies anymore."

"I think you should go back to the house now, Chizzy."

Chizzy spread her plump little hands on the table in front of her as if she were counting her fingers to make sure they were all there. "Something's happened."

"I don't know."

"Something's happened," she repeated, and it was not a question but a simple statement of fact. She had ten fingers, something had happened.

Michael walked quickly through the avocado grove down to the creek. Here, civilization seemed miles away. Yet its sounds reverberated up and down the canyon, the insistent whine and roar of a power saw, the rhythmic tap of a hammer, a plane heading for the airport, the shouts of children playing in the distance.

Children, Michael thought. Firenze hated children. They were out to get her. They blew down at her from trees, they floated through the air like kites.

He began picking his way upstream as fast as he could, crossing and recrossing the creek to avoid barbed shrubs and poison oak. The wind, which had been brisk in the morning, then died down during the day, was coming up again as the afternoon wore on. The eucalyptus trees shook their tousled heads in frenzy and pelted the intruder with pods as hard as rocks. Jays swooped in front of him, squawking, and when he called Dru's name the acorn woodpeckers answered, correcting him.

"Dru! Dru!"

"Jacob, Jacob, Jacob."

"Dru."

"Jacob."

The sycamore trees were the commonest along the creek, their leaves the gaudiest and noisiest, their mottled gray bark the most compelling to the eye. But the live oak trees were the most ancient and durable natives. Their massive trunks were studded with acorns fitted into holes pecked out by the woodpeckers. During fall and winter a few leaves dropped to the ground but most of them remained on the tree to shelter hundreds of small birds at night and during storms.

It was under one of the largest of these oaks that Annamay had been found in a patch of poison oak covered with debris. The area was easy to find now because it had been cleared, the poison oak sprayed with herbicide and hauled away along with all the other dead and dying vegetation.

He stood in the clearing and looked up into the oak tree and saw what he had hoped and prayed he would not see. About thirty-five or forty feet above the ground Dru was clinging facedown to one of the limbs. She was as motionless as if she had grown out of the bark like a new kind of fungus.

He called to her. "Dru, don't look down. It's a friend of yours, Michael. I've come to help you. Do you hear me?"

She did not respond and he realized she was frozen with fear and that even if he succeeded in reaching her he probably couldn't loosen her grip and bring her down safely. He would need the assistance of experts.

"Listen to me, Dru. I'm going for help. I'll be back in a few minutes. Don't panic and don't look down."

He kept yelling at her as he scrambled up the hillside to the nearest house.

"I'm bringing help. . . . Don't look down. . . . I'll be right back."

When he reached the house at the top of the hill he pounded on the back door with his fist. The door remained closed but a woman's voice spoke to him through a partly opened window.

"Go away."

"I must use your phone to call Emergency."

"Boss lady say no open door, no talk strangers."

He couldn't identify her exact nationality from her voice, but she was of Hispanic origin. He used the only Spanish he knew, the street language he'd picked up at his old parish in East Los Angeles:

"Llame a emergencia, nueve-uno-uno, y dígales que una niña está strapada en un árbol al fondo de una zanja. Y deles su dirección. ¿Entendio? Llame al nueve-uno-uno."

He didn't wait for her response. He had to assume she would do as she was told because he knew he must hurry back to the child in the oak tree.

Dru had not moved.

"I'm coming up to get you, Dru. Don't be afraid. The fire department will be here in a few minutes with ladders that will reach all the way up to where you are." *I hope. I don't know how far their ladders extend.*

He began to climb the tree. He had never had time for athletics in his high school years and he couldn't remember climbing a tree even when he was Dru's age. But he kept on trying, talking as he moved.

"You know how the fire department rescues kittens when they're caught up trees or telephone poles? That's what they're coming to do for you. All you have to do is stay cool and not look down."

The bark of the tree was rough and his hands were the soft hands of a man who'd lived by brain not brawn. They were bleeding before he was ten feet off the ground.

"Pretend you are a kitten, Dru. Kittens are curious, they like to explore like little girls, and sometimes they get into trouble and have to be rescued. Pretend you are a kitten, Dru. Do you like kittens?"

He was still too far away to tell for sure whether his words were having any effect or not, but he felt she was listening. She had moved her head slightly in his direction.

"I bet you like kittens. Maybe you even have one of your own. Do you?"

She spoke for the first time, a single word that seemed to have no connection with what he'd been saying. He wondered if she had really flipped. The word sounded like marmalade.

If she had flipped she might be incapable of obeying instructions from either him or the firemen. She might lose her grip on the limb involuntarily or make a sudden decision to jump.

He needed something to keep her securely fastened to the limb until she could be reached. He wasn't wearing a belt which probably wouldn't have been long enough anyway. But he was wearing the wool sweater Lorna's aunt had knitted for him one Christmas. Like all her gifts the sweater had a basic flaw originating with the giver. It had apparently been designed for a much taller man (the kind she probably thought Lorna should have married). The sleeves were several inches too long. From the end of one to the end of the other it measured at least six feet, and the woolen fibers were as strong as hemp.

As soon as he took the sweater off he realized it had more potential than he'd thought. For the rest of his ascent he used it as a combination security blanket and rope, throwing it over each successive limb and pulling himself up. When he reached the level of the child he saw that her lips were moving.

"Are you trying to tell me something, Dru? I can't understand you."

"Marmalady."

"All right, you can have some marmalade as soon as we get you down."

She opened her eyes briefly, then closed them again. Her school uniform was torn, her knees scraped and her cheeks bleeding where she had pressed her face against the rough bark.

"I saw her," she said. "I saw her down there."

"There's no one down there, Dru."

"There was before. I saw Annamay."

"That was a long time ago."

"She got up and walked away."

"She made sounds when she was falling?"

"They were happy sounds, like she was learning to fly."

She screamed, Michael thought. *She screamed like a banshee and Firenze heard her, and saw her falling out of the tree.*

"I didn't want her to come along," Dru said. "I was going to practice mountain climbing so I could go with my boyfriend Kevin when we grow up. She was a nuisance. I told her to go home. You're such a baby, I told her, and you're never going to be a mountain climber like me and Kevin because you're scared of things."

Her words were interspersed with sobs. He kept edging along the limb toward her. He could hear in the distance the sounds of a siren and a whelper. A flood of relief and of gratitude swept over him, gratitude to Lorna's aunt for the sweater, to the oak tree for its strength, to the maid who'd called the emergency number and to the firemen who were responding.

"Can you hear the sirens, Dru? Those are the men who are coming to rescue you. You're going to be fine. All you have to do is keep from looking down and I think you can."

"I don't know."

"Listen to me now, Dru. Do you know what mountain climbers do when they're caught in a dangerous situation? They secure themselves with ropes. You and I don't have any ropes so we'll use this sweater. I'm going to tie it around your waist. Like this."

She offered no resistance as he put the sweater around the limb and under her arms, then tied it at the back with a square knot. "You're going to be all right now, Dru. The firemen will bring you down the ladder and take you home."

"I don't want to go home. They'll blame me for letting

her climb the tree. They'll blame me because Annamay's younger and prettier than me. I'm not going home. Never. I'm going to wait here for Annamay to come back."

"Dru—"

"I won't listen to you."

"Yes, you will," Michael said. "She's not coming back. She died when she hit the ground."

"But she got up and walked away, laughing." The child repeated the words over and over like a magic spell she used to defeat the truth.

But the power of the spell was gone, and each time she said it it sounded weaker like a fading echo.

I've been chasing a monster, Michael thought, *and come up with a mouse, this mouse of a child who watched her friend die and was so shocked and terrified she had to pretend it never happened.*

"She isn't coming back?" Dru said.

"No."

Tears started rolling down her cheeks, washing away the blood and dirt, leaving clean little paths.